Across the Screen

A REMOTE OFFICE ROMANCE

I0600207

By Elaine Lawrence

CHAPTER ONE

It was almost midnight when Ava realized she was laughing too hard at something that wasn't actually that funny. Which meant she was well past the point she should've ended her call with Cole Maddox, her coworker.

[Ava]: Get a grip, Ava. It's not that funny. He's just stupidly charming in high definition.

His face filled the tiny Teams window on her screen—hoodie rumpled, headset skewed, hair doing that wavy thing she tried not to notice. His smile was annoyingly perfect, his features softened by the glow of his monitor.

Cole typed the final line, merged the bug-fix branch into the live environment, and watched the tests turn green. He let out a breath and looked over at her.

"Okay, Ava," he said with a smirk. "I told you about my disaster of a date this week, and you enjoyed it way too much. So come on—what was your weekly mess?"

This was how it had always been with them. Five years of working together without ever meeting in person. Just calls, screen shares, and chat messages that stretched well past business hours. Their remote late-night sessions felt like a little world of their own, their banter skimming the line between friendly and something warmer.

Ava dropped her forehead into her palm. "Can we not? This one was... bad."

Cole leaned back, smug grin widening. "Oh, come on, I told you about the aquarium disaster."

"You bumped into your date and knocked her into the kiddie pool, but mine is worse," she said flatly.

He rubbed his jaw. "Yeah... she didn't take it well."

[Ava]: Understatement of the year. He'd probably traumatized a group of toddlers... and a stingray.

She snorted. "You don't say."

"So...?" he drawled, entirely too charming.

She rolled her eyes before glancing down at her keyboard.

Cole leaned forward in his chair, lips curling into a soft smile. "How bad? Like normal-Ava-date bad, or the kind where I should prepare a sympathy card?"

She lifted her head just enough to glare.

"Somewhere between 'run' and 'burn my phone.' He called himself a 'digital nomad' and then asked if my remote job meant I lived in a van."

Cole winced. "Oof. That's a felony-level red flag."

"And he said it with confidence," she added. "Like it was a compliment."

"That's impressive even for you," he teased. "Your talent for attracting chaos is honestly heroic."

"Cole, it's late," she said, gathering her long, wavy chestnut hair into a messy bun. "The hotfix has been deployed, and the project is back on track. I have a flight in eight hours, I need sleep."

Her oversized pajama shirt slipped off one shoulder. She tugged it back up without thinking, but Cole noticed. His gaze flicked down, then away, a tiny catch in his breath she might've missed if she hadn't been looking at him.

[Ava]: Did he...? No. Don't be weird. It's just fabric plus gravity.

On his side of the call, Cole swallowed and forced his gaze back to the error log.

[Cole]: Do not look again. She's your coworker, not a thirst trap. Focus, Cole. Code, not collarbone.

"The time wouldn't be a problem if you would just stay at a hotel next to the airport the night before a flight, like me," he said, clearing his throat. "I seriously don't understand how you can be organized in your work life but not in your personal one. I bet you haven't even packed yet."

His words dipped into that soft Louisiana curve—the one that only showed up on late-night calls when he was tired.

Ava felt her pulse jump, which was ridiculous. Completely, absolutely absurd. But she couldn't help it. That tiny slip of accent had become one of her favorite things about late-night troubleshooting.

Not that she'd ever admit that out loud. Ever.

Ava rolled her eyes. "Not everyone is a planning robot like you, and for your information, I am mostly packed."

[Ava]: If three shirts on the bed and a pile of panic count as mostly.

"I prefer efficient adult," he corrected with a smirk.

"Same thing."

He let out a soft laugh—too soft, too real—and something warm fluttered in her chest.

[Ava]: Oh no. Absolutely not. We do not flutter over coworkers. That's how people end up in HR training videos.

"I'll see you in the monthly meeting next week," he said. "Safe travels, Ava."

The meeting ended before she could say goodbye.

Cole stared at his now-empty screen for a beat longer than necessary.

[Cole]: Next week. Why does that feel farther away than it is? It's just a meeting. It's always just a meeting.

At least, that's what he told himself while his mind queued up a highlight reel of every moment she'd made those meetings anything but ordinary.

Ava sank back in her oversized office chair, letting it spin lazily as she stared at her reflection in the dark monitor.

[Ava]: Why is it so easy to lose track of time with him? It's work talk. And meme sharing. And that thing he does when he laughs with his whole face...

She shook it off, shut down her laptop, and finished packing. She told herself she wasn't nervous about the flight, or the wedding, or the fact that Cole's voice still echoed in her mind.

She was lying.

[Ava]: You're nervous about all three. Congratulations. You're a walking anxiety smoothie.

Beep. Beep. Beep.

Ava groaned, turned off her alarm, and tossed her phone across the bed. Morning had arrived with the subtlety of a freight train.

[Ava]: Ten more minutes wouldn't kill anyone. Planes wait for good people, right?

She showered, pulled on comfy travel clothes, and hauled her suitcase outside just as her Uber arrived. Halfway to SEA-TAC, her phone rang.

"Hello."

"Hey girl, when are you getting here? I don't know how much more I can take," Brittany wailed the moment Ava answered.

"Calm down and breathe. What's going on?" Ava asked.

Brittany exhaled shakily. Ava could practically hear the freezer door opening.

[Ava]: Either grabbing ice cream or a frozen pizza. Or both. Crisis levels confirmed.

"My mother is losing her mind. L-o-s-i-n-g. She wants to redo the seating chart two days before the wedding. And she keeps asking if I've gained weight. Like I'm going to bust out of my dress on Sunday."

Ava sighed. "Deep breaths, Britt. She's stressed, not malicious. She means well."

"I know," Brittany groaned, spoon scraping loudly against an ice cream carton. "I'm just glad you're coming early." Then a sly shift in her tone. "I really thought you and Maddox would hit it off if you hadn't let my mom set you up with her friend's son."

Ava blinked. "Who?"

"Remember? I told you—he and Zach are best friends? The one you always miss when you visit. I swear if you two ever actually met—"

"Britt, I let your mom set me up with Tony, so she'd stop grilling you," Ava cut in. "I didn't realize it came with a lecture."

Brittany groaned. "Tony is fine, Ava. But Maddox—"

"I gotta go. Boarding soon," Ava lied. "See you soon."

She hung up and inhaled deeply.

[Ava]: *I'm a grown woman. I can do this. It's just air travel. With strangers. And turbulence. And possibly lost luggage and—*

"Stop it," she muttered.

[Ava]: *Yes, good. Tell the anxiety to stop. That always works.*

Security was a nightmare.

Her bag was flagged for a forgotten water bottle. She tripped over her own foot and nearly face-planted into the lap of an incredibly attractive man putting his shoes on.

"Oh my god, I am so sorry," she squeaked, embarrassed.

He grabbed her elbow to steady her. "Whoa there," he said with a slow smile. "I usually buy a lady dinner first."

[Ava]: *Of course, the first man I practically tackle is a cringeworthy walking flirt.*

"I'm Adam," he added, holding her arm just a hair too long.

"Great. Wonderful. Bye," she blurted, pulling away.

[Ava]: Abort mission, Ava. Do not engage with an airport flirt man. You have enough chaos scheduled for today.

She had no idea this was only the first disaster of the day.

She reached her gate just as they called final boarding. As she stepped onto the plane, she caught a glimpse of Adam boarding behind her.

Perfect.
Exactly what she needed.

[Ava]: The universe really said: "You know what she needs? A recurring side character."

Thankfully, he sat in the row in front of her—but that didn't stop him from twisting around to attempt conversation until she aggressively slid her headphones on.

The flight itself wasn't terrible. No turbulence. No screaming children. No more humiliation.

[Ava]: This is fine. You're fine. See? Planes sometimes stay in the air.

When they landed early in Chicago, Ava could've cried with relief. Maybe—just maybe—today would go her way.

Then she looked at the departure board.
Her connecting flight flashed red:

Cancelled.

"No," she whispered.

[Ava]: There it is. The twist. Of course.

Passengers swarmed the gate desk. Ava joined the line, hugging her carry-on anxiously.

"This is unacceptable!" A familiar voice thundered across the terminal.

Adam.
Of course.

[Ava]: Oh, good. Airport Flirt is back and being a total jerk. Love that for me.

He was berating the gate agent like she personally dismantled the plane. The woman looked exhausted and seconds away from tears.

A tall man stepped forward—broad shoulders, dark wavy hair escaping his hood. A warm, clean scent drifted toward her—something like cedar soap and late-night coffee.

"Hey. She's doing her job. Back off."

Adam spun. "Who the hell are you?"

"A guy who doesn't like bullies."

[Ava]: That voice... no way. No actual way.

Adam stormed off.

As the man turned around, his eyes found Ava. Everything around her dropped away.

"Ava?"

Her breath caught. "Cole?"

[Ava]: You have got to be kidding me. The universe really said: surprise, bitch.

His eyes softened in a way she had never seen through a screen. "Wow. You... you're real."

[Cole]: Of course she's real, idiot. Say something normal. Don't tell her she looks different in 3D.

She laughed—too loud, too shaky. "Debatable."

"What are you doing here?" he asked softly, stepping closer before hesitating.

[Cole]: Don't hug her. Don't grab her. You are in an airport, not a rom-com trailer.

"Not flying, obviously," she said with a weak attempt at sass.

He froze, realizing he'd nearly pulled her into a hug without thinking, again.

[Cole]: Control it. You don't get to touch her because you've thought about it.

They stepped aside, the chaos of the airport fading into a strange, quiet bubble.

"Britt is going to kill me," Ava muttered.

[Ava]: Britt is going to scream so loud the Midwest will hear.

"Your friend will understand. This isn't your fault," Cole said gently, shoving his hands into his pockets as if fighting the urge to reach for her again.

"But I don't know what to do now—where to stay, if I'll make it on time—" Ava's breath hitched as panic rose.

[Ava]: Hotel. Rebooking. Lost luggage. Wedding meltdown. Oh God, I'm going to pass out next to a Cinnabon.

Without thinking, Cole pulled her to him. Her cheek pressed against his chest as she breathed in his scent—warm, clean, impossible to forget.

"Don't worry," he murmured. "We've managed worse on a deadline. We've got this."

[Cole]: You just hugged her, no, this is more than a hug, you are holding her...close. In public. In an airport. But she's shaking. You couldn't not.

[Ava]: This smell should be illegal on coworkers. This warmth shouldn't be allowed. This is not HR-approved behavior,

Ava thought frantically as she pulled back.

"Oh shit—I'm so sorry, Ava," Cole blurted, flustered. "I didn't mean to make you uncomfortable. It was just instinct—you looked upset."

[Cole]: Too much. Too fast. Good job, Cole, grab your coworker like you're in a drama.

"It's... it's okay, Cole. Really. Thank you."

[Ava]: Pull it together. Stop melting. He was just being nice. Very... chest-forward nice.

They got back in line, standing dangerously close but just far enough apart.

Cole nudged her. "So, what has you traveling today?"

"Wedding," Ava said, a small smile tugging at her mouth.

"Wedding," he said. "Same."

Her brows lifted. "I guess it really is wedding season."

"Especially in New York," Cole said. "I had to turn down a couple, but not this one."

His smile tipped warmer. "The groom's my best friend."

Ava's expression softened. "Mine too. And apparently her mom has reached level ten chaos mode."

Neither of them was paying enough attention to notice the coincidence. Ava is flying out to her best friend Brittany's wedding, and Cole is heading to be the best man at his best friend's wedding. Same city. Same weekend.

But with the air still humming from that warm too comforting hug, neither of them connected the dots. They both smiled, unaware of just how entangled their travels were.

The gate agent handed them hotel and meal vouchers. Their new flight leaves tomorrow at noon.

Ava groaned. "Now what?"

"Hey," Cole said with a soft smile. "We'll survive this. Teamwork, remember?"

[Cole]: Say "teamwork" like it doesn't feel completely different in person.

They walked toward the shuttle, hands brushing occasionally, each touch sending a little zap through Ava's nerves.

[Ava]: Stop noticing every physics-based accident as "chemistry," brain.

"So..." Cole said, hands sliding into his pockets.

"Hotel... then dinner? On the voucher?"

Ava smirked. "Only if you don't judge my food choices."

"No promises."

[Cole]: She's even prettier in bad airport lighting. That's unfair. And extremely unhelpful.

The shuttle pulled up. Cole gestured for her to go first.

"Ladies first," he said, voice low and warm.

As she stepped up into the shuttle, his hand found the small of her back, steady and instinctive.

A shiver ran through her.

[Ava]: Nope. Not reacting. Totally chill. Just going to pretend my spine didn't just hum.

Cole stepped in behind her. "Guess we're stuck together for the night, Ava."

Her pulse jumped.

[Ava]: Do not picture that sentence out of context. Do. Not.

She had no idea how right he was.

CHAPTER TWO

As they got off the shuttle, their hands brushed when Cole reached for her suitcase. Both froze. Their eyes met for a moment that felt too long before he stepped back.

[Cole]: Don't grab her hand. Don't be that guy. Just carry the suitcase and behave like a professional adult.

The lobby was packed with stranded travelers. The noise, the movement, the bright lights—

Ava's chest tightened.
Her breath shortened.

"Blue walls... white flowers... gold tiles..." she whispered, grounding herself.

[Ava]: Count the things. Blue, white, and gold. In. Out. Do not spiral in the Hilton lobby, please.

Cole must have sensed it. He gently took her arm and guided her to a quieter corner.

"Sit," he murmured, as he knelt down in front of her. He touched her cheek lightly, eyes locked on hers. "Just breathe with me. In... one, two, three. Out... one, two, three..."

[Cole]: There you are.

He thought, watching her pupils slowly steady.

[Cole]: You're okay. I've got you. Just like a production issue—slow it down, step by step.

Her panic melted under the weight of his voice, his touch, his presence.

"Stay right here," he said once her breathing steadied. "I'll get our rooms."

Ava managed a nod. "Mmhm."

[Ava]: Get it fucking together, Ava. This is your coworker. This is Cole. You have known him for literally years. We are going our separate ways tomorrow. Get. It. Together.

She watched him at the counter—steady, calm, composed—and her mind slipped into dangerous territory.

[Ava]: He's actually... kind of ridiculously good in emergencies. That shouldn't be attractive. And yet.

He returned, towering over her slightly as she stood.

"Well," he said, eyes flicking over her before he caught himself, "there's good news and bad news."

"Let's have it."

"We got the last room—"

"Last room? As in one room?" she cut in.

"Yes," he said quickly, "but if you let me finish… it's a suite, and our vouchers mostly covered it, and there's a couch…" He hesitated. "But if you'd rather, I can stay in the lobby. I can get some work done anyway."

[Cole]: I'll sleep in a potted plant if it makes you feel safe. Just say the word.

Ava swallowed. "Don't be ridiculous Cole, as long as there are two beds, it's fine."

[Cole]: And if there aren't?

A soft smile pulled at his mouth.

[Cole]: No. Don't finish that thought.

The elevator door slid open, and Cole stepped aside, holding the door with one arm.

"After you," he said, voice warm enough to make her knees flicker.

Ava stepped past him, gripping her suitcase too tightly. The space felt smaller than it should have—much smaller—and suddenly she was acutely aware of being sealed in a metal box with Cole Maddox.

Her heart pounded in her ears.

[Ava]: It's just an elevator. A very tall, broad, unfairly good-smelling elevator companion.

Cole pressed the button for the fourteenth floor.

Silence fell.
Not peaceful silence.

Heavy.
Charged.
Hyperaware.

Cole shifted beside her, the brush of his jacket against her arm sending heat up her spine. He cleared his throat.

"So... uh... elevators," he said.

Ava blinked. "Elevators?"

"Yeah. Small. Very... elevator-y."

A laugh escaped her. "Wow. Incredible observation. Intense stuff."

He shot her a wounded look. "Look, I'm trying here. My brain is... not working normally."

[Cole]: Because all it's doing is cataloguing how close you are. Great job, brain.

"Is that different from usual?" she teased.

He gave her a crooked smile. "Funny."

Their eyes held a beat too long.
Dangerous.

Ava tore her gaze away, staring at the floor numbers.

10…

11…

[Ava]: Any slower and I'm filing a complaint with gravity.

"You okay?" he asked quietly.

"Define okay."

He huffed a soft laugh. "Fair."

"Ava…?" His voice dropped. "Back there… at the gate. I didn't mean to grab you."

She kept her eyes forward. "You were helping. It's okay."

"That's the thing," he said quietly. "I didn't think. I just reacted. And I don't want you thinking I—not that I—"

[Cole]: Don't say "wanted to." Don't make it worse. She doesn't need your feelings on top of everything else.

"Cole," she cut in gently, "it's fine. Really."

He nodded once, jaw tightening like he wanted to say more but wouldn't.

"Okay," he murmured. "We'll leave it there."

But the silence after that said they absolutely did not.

[Cole]: Big liar energy, Cole. Good job.

Ding.
The doors opened.

Cole stepped out first, pausing as if waiting for her. "Come on. Let's see our... room."

The word *our* hit her like a live wire.

[Ava]: Abort mission. No. Stay calm. This is fine. Totally fine. Completely not fine.

They walked down the carpeted hallway, the wheels of their suitcases whispering over the floor. Cole stopped at the very end, sliding the keycard into the lock.

For half a second, Ava imagined opening the door to one enormous bed.

[Ava]: If there's only one bed, I am throwing myself out the nearest window. Politely.

The lock beeped. Cole pushed the door open and stepped aside.

"Aft—" He caught himself, swallowing. "Uh. Go ahead."

She rolled her suitcase in and stopped.

The suite was small but nice: a queen bed against one wall, a pull-out couch, a tiny table, and a window overlooking a parking lot full of stranded lives.

Relief loosened something in her chest.

[Ava]: Thank you, hospitality gods—two separate sleep surfaces. We live to be semi-professional another day.

"Okay," Cole said, stepping in behind her, voice going into that calm, decisive register he used on production calls. "You take the bed. I'll grab the couch."

He said it like a done deal, like there was no other configuration in the universe.

Ava spun around. "What? No. You're taller. You take the bed, I'll—"

He shook his head immediately. "Not happening."

[Cole]: No way am I letting you sleep on a pull-out after the day you just had. I'm not a monster.

"Cole—"

"Ava," he said gently, but firmly. "I'm fine on the couch. I've crashed on worse. Like, significantly worse."

She narrowed her eyes at him. "You're just saying that to be nice."

"Yeah," he said. "And also because it's true."

[Cole]: Please don't argue with me on this. I already held you in an airport today. Let me at least nail basic human decency.

She hesitated, fingers tightening on her suitcase handle.

[Ava]: If you keep refusing, you're basically saying you don't trust him to be a decent human. And you do. Maybe too much.

"Are you sure?" she asked quietly.

His expression softened. "Absolutely."

He smiled, small but warm, and something in her finally unclenched.

"...Okay," she said. "You win. I'll take the bed."

[Ava]: And I will overthink what that means for the rest of my natural life.

Cole nodded once, like a commander satisfied with a successful negotiation. "Good."

He dropped his suitcase near the dresser and moved toward the couch, tugging at the back cushions to check how they unfolded. "See? Perfect. Luxury accommodations."

"It squeaks when you look at it," she said.

"Same," he deadpanned.

A laugh escaped her before she could stop it.

[Ava]: Why is he like this? Why does it work?

Ava set her bag by the bed, trying not to picture him stretched out on the too-small pull out.

[Ava]: It's fine. He offered. You didn't force him. He's an adult. A very broad-shouldered, probably-going-to-be-cramped adult.

Cole glanced around the room like he needed something to do with his hands. "So... we haven't eaten."

Her stomach chose that exact moment to growl, loud and pathetic.

"Apparently, my body agrees," she muttered.

He smiled, and it felt like the room warmed by a few degrees. "Want to use the vouchers? There's a restaurant downstairs. Airport-adjacent cuisine. Very fancy."

[Ava]: Say yes. It's just dinner. With your coworker, who is sharing a hotel suite with you. Totally normal. Sure. Let's all pretend that's normal.

"Yeah," she said. "Dinner sounds good."

"Cool." He gestured toward the door. "Give me five minutes to look less like I lost a fight with O'Hare, and we'll go?"

"Same," she said quickly.

[Ava]: Right. Freshen up. Fix your face. Pretend you didn't nearly melt into him in the lobby and then accept his bed like some Regency heroine.

He grabbed a clean hoodie from his bag and disappeared into the bathroom. Ava sat on the edge of the bed for a second, staring at the closed door.

[Ava]: This is fine. Totally fine. Completely not fine.

They walked to the tiny hotel restaurant, shoulders brushing once, twice, again—each time followed by a tiny, silent apology neither voiced.

Dinner unfolded in a blur of shared plates and half-finished thoughts. Cole leaned in to mutter commentary about the menu. She nudged his leg under the table when he made her laugh mid-bite.

The conversation never stalled. It slipped and looped, familiar as muscle memory, like this wasn't their first evening out but one of many.

[Ava]: How is it even better in person? That feels unfair. I did not emotionally prepare for upgraded banter.

At one point, she laughed so hard she snorted.

Cole choked on his drink.
They froze.

"Never speak of that again," she warned.

"Absolutely speaking of it again," he promised.

[Cole]: I'd listen to that sound on a loop. God, that's pathetic.

An older couple passed by and smiled. "You two are adorable."

Ava and Cole locked eyes.

"Coworkers," they said in unison—way too quickly.

The couple winked, entirely unconvinced.

[Ava]: Great. Even strangers can see the chaos vibes.

If anything, dinner made everything worse. Or better. Depending on how reckless you wanted to be.

Every time he laughed, that stupid dimple appeared. Every time she smiled, his gaze dropped to her lips for a fraction longer than necessary.

[Cole]: *Stop staring at her mouth. You're not subtle. She's going to notice.*

Every time their knees bumped under the table... neither moved.

She leaned in without thinking.
He mirrored her instantly.

Their faces inched closer—

The server appeared with the check and Ava practically levitated out of the booth.

[Ava]: *Thank you, random server. I was about half a second from catastrophic life choices.*

Back in the suite, Cole peeled off his hoodie, revealing a fitted T-shirt that should've violated three HR policies. On camera, he'd always seemed harmless. Boyish even.

Not like this.

He moved closer to drop the hoodie on the couch and didn't stop when he knew he should have. One smaller step followed, instinctive, drawn by the quiet pull between them.

His gaze caught hers. Held.
The air shifted. Tightened.

Ava's pulse stumbled.

She turned away, grasping for the nearest excuse.

A lamp.

[Ava]: Yes, this is absolutely the most fascinating lamp I've ever seen. Definitely not avoiding the almost indecent way that T-shirt clings to his arms, outlining muscles he has no business having. Not at all.

"Nice lamp inspection," Cole snorted.

"Shut up."

[Ava]: Abort. Hide in the bathroom. Reboot your brain.

She escaped to the bathroom, changed into leggings and a soft T-shirt, then gave herself a silent pep talk.

[Ava]: Coworkers. He is your coworker. Just walk out there and go to bed. No flirting. No accidental cuddling. No kissing his stupid mouth.

When she stepped out, Cole froze.

His eyes swept over her once, slow enough to short-circuit her brain, before he snapped back to neutral.

[Ava]: Leggings were a mistake. Why are leggings legal?

"I-uh—you look... comfortable," he said, voice rougher.

"You too," she whispered.

He wiggled his eyebrows. "Checking out the merch?"

"Jesus Christ, Cole."

[Cole]: If she rolls her eyes at you one more time, you're deservedly doomed.

He laughed and tossed a pillow at her. "You walked right into that one."

She threw it back, hitting his chest.

He caught it—and went still.
Heat flickered in the air between them.

Just a moment.
Just long enough to feel it.

[Cole]: Don't close the distance. Don't be that guy. Do not be that guy.

"Okay," she whispered. "Sleep."

"Yep," he said too quickly. "Sleep. We're totally doing that."

He turned off the light.

Darkness settled.
Sharper than the room had been before.

Ava lay in bed, staring at the ceiling, acutely aware of Cole just feet away on the pull-out couch.

Every shift he made.
Every slow exhale.

Every thought she absolutely should not be having.

[Ava]: Stop picturing what he looks like without that T-shirt. Please stop it. Go to sleep, you menace.

A long, heavy beat.
Then soft in the dark.

"Ava... are you awake?"

Her breath caught.

[Ava]: Oh. Dangerous question.

"...Yeah."

A pause pressed against her ribs.

"Okay," he whispered. "Good pillows?"

Not what she expected.
Not what she wanted.

"Um... yeah," she said with a tiny laugh. "They're nice."

"Mine are nice too. Well—goodnight," he said. "Hope you sleep well."

[Cole]: Really? Good pillows? That is all you got?

Ava rolled onto her side, facing the vague warmth coming from his direction, and let out a soft, helpless breath.

Neither of them slept more than a moment.

CHAPTER THREE

Ava came awake to the soft morning light, the hum of the hotel AC, and a bladder that felt like it was about to declare a medical emergency.

She bolted upright. The room was quiet except for—

The shower.
Running.
Loudly.

Then horror dawned.

[Ava]: Oh no. No. This is it. This is how your dignity dies.

She hopped out of bed, legs crossed like a panicked toddler, and shuffled to the bathroom door. Steam curled from underneath it.

Ava knocked frantically. "Cole? Cole, I—uh—I need in there."

The water shut off instantly.

"You okay?" His voice was muffled, low, still raspy with sleep.

[Ava]: Of course, his morning voice is illegal.

"No! Yes! But... no!" She was practically dancing. "I... I need to pee!"

A pause.

"Ava... like... right now?"

"Yes, right now! This is a code red situation!"

She heard him laugh—an actual laugh, warm and low in his chest.

"Okay, give me thirty seconds."

"I don't have thirty seconds!"

"Ten?"

"I don't—just—yes. Ten!"

A frantic rustling, a thump, a curse, then the door cracked open just enough for her to squeeze through without seeing anything she shouldn't.

Except she absolutely saw something she shouldn't.

Cole stood there, half-dressed, towel low on his hips, shirt clutched in his hands, dark hair dripping down his temples.

[Ava]: Nope. Absolutely not. That's... those are abs. Real ones. With definition. I'm in danger.

Ava slapped a hand over her eyes like a Victorian woman fainting. "Nope! Too early. Too much. I'm blind."

He snorted. "You're fine. I'm decent."

[Ava]: You are a walking HR violation right now.

"You are absolutely not decent!" she squeaked as she darted past him and slammed the door behind her.

He chuckled. "You're welcome."

[Cole]: You did not just say "you're welcome," you smug bastard.

"For what? Emotional trauma?"

"For letting you pee."

"Okay, that's fair," she admitted.

[Ava]: Bare minimum hero, but sure.

When she emerged five minutes later—freshly mortified—Cole was fully dressed, sitting on the edge of the pull-out couch, tying his shoes like a normal civilized adult.

Unlike her.

His eyes lifted. "Crisis averted?"

"Barely," she muttered, cheeks still burning. "Thanks."

"No problem." He stood. "I'll always rescue you from bathroom emergencies."

[Cole]: Could you sound less charmed by her, maybe? Anything? No? Okay.

"Don't make that a thing."

"It's already a thing."

"I hate you."

"You don't."

She swallowed. "Unfortunately."

His smile softened, and she had to look away.

[Cole]: Don't read into that. Do not read into that.

By the time their bags were packed, Ava had already tripped over her suitcase twice, walked into the suite doorframe once, and dropped her granola bar on the carpet before picking it up and eating it anyway because she had no dignity left.

Cole watched the granola incident with barely concealed amusement.

"Five-second rule," she announced defensively.

"We're in a hotel," he said. "That's... brave."

"It wasn't the part on the floor that I'm eating," she lied.

"Uh-huh."

[Cole]: She's going to get hotel carpet disease, and somehow, I'll feel responsible.

In the shuttle, Ava nearly fell into his lap when the driver hit a pothole. She grabbed the nearest thing—which happened to be Cole's forearm.

His very warm, very muscular forearm.

[Ava]: Oh. Oh, no. That's solid. That's so solid. Abort!

She snatched her hand back so fast she smacked herself in the stomach.

Cole winced for her. "You okay there, champ?"

"Totally fine," she wheezed.

"Right." He tried not to smile. Failed.

[Cole]: She's going to kill me one day with secondhand embarrassment, and I'll die smiling.

Ava glared at the window, silently blaming gravity for all her misfortunes.

[Ava]: Gravity is out to get me. Science is personal now.

Security was better. Slightly.

Ava managed to drop her boarding pass (twice), walk into one of those rope dividers and apologize to a trash can she bumped into.

Cole watched all of this with the fond expression of someone trying not to laugh.

[Cole]: *She apologized to a trash can. Of course she did. How is this person also terrifyingly good at process mapping?*

When she finished putting her shoes back on, he leaned down.

"You good?"

"No one died," she said. "So I consider that a win."

"Low bar."

"It's the only bar I'm capable of clearing today."

He chuckled. "You cleared the one in the lobby."

"Barely."

[Cole]: *And I really wanted to pick you up and carry you out of there, which is... not a normal coworker thought.*

Their gate was quiet. Too quiet.

Ava eyed it suspiciously. "Something's wrong."

Cole shook his head. "Ava, everything's fine."

"Don't say that."

"Why?"

"Because the universe hears confidence as a challenge."

He opened his mouth—probably to argue—but then their plane began boarding early.

Ava pointed. "See? That's suspicious."

"It's... called being on schedule."

"No. Something's coming."

He sighed. "You're impossible."

"Correct."

[Cole]: And yet I'd still choose your chaos over a typical day with anyone else. That's the problem.

Ava took the window seat. Cole took the aisle. A middle-aged businessman sat between them, wearing noise-canceling headphones and an expression that said I regret booking this flight.

Ava buckled her seatbelt.

Cole leaned forward behind the businessman's shoulder. "You okay?"

"I will be if this plane stays in the air."

He grinned. "So... maybe."

"Not funny."

"Kinda funny."

She rolled her eyes—but couldn't fight a smile.

The businessman cleared his throat loudly. "You two want to switch seats so you can flirt without leaning over me?"

Ava made a sound that could only be described as a dying, breathy squeak. "We're not—he's not—we're just coworkers."

"Oh," the man said, nodding slowly in the way people do when they very much do not believe you. "Sure you are."

Cole coughed violently, like he had inhaled his own dignity.

[Ava]: Stranger danger, but make it accurate.

The flight was a masterclass in accidental intimacy.

Cole passed her his cookie without looking at her, sliding it past the businessman like a covert operation.

[Cole]: If she doesn't take this cookie, I'm going to be weirdly offended.

40

She stole it like she was smuggling state secrets.

He caught her smoothing out a wrinkle in her napkin and said, "I think that's the most Virgo thing I've ever seen you do."

"I'm not a Virgo."

"You have Virgo energy."

"What does that even mean?"

"You alphabetize your apps."

She gasped. "How do you know that?"

"You shared your screen once on Teams." He grinned. "You put the weather app in the 'W' folder."

"It belongs there!"

The businessman sighed and turned up the volume on his headphones.

[Cole]: We deserve that.

During landing, Ava grabbed the armrests hard enough to almost leave indentations.

Cole braced one hand lightly on the back of the businessman's seat and leaned in. "You're okay. Easiest part."

"Liar," she muttered through clenched teeth.

He laughed softly. "I got you."

[Ava]: I wish that didn't feel like more than a casual reassurance.

The plane touched down as smoothly as butter.

Ava blinked. "Oh."

"Told you."

"Shut up."

[Cole]: She's cute when she's wrong. Don't say that out loud.

Outside the airport, the chaos was immediate. Cars honked. People shouted. Suitcases rolled across uneven pavement.

Ava's Uber pulled up the exact moment Cole's did.

He shifted his suitcase to his other hand, looking... hesitant. Almost conflicted.

[Cole]: Say something. Don't let this be a weird fade-to-black.

"Well," he said quietly, "I have to go...pick up my tux."

"Tux?" Ava repeated, trying not to overanalyze the minor ache she felt. "You'll look... nice."

[Ava]: Nice. Great word choice. Very safe.

Ten out of ten, no notes, absolutely lying.

His smile flickered, faint and warm. "Thanks. And you? Off to handle wedding emergencies?"

"Yep. I'm the bride's emotional support human."

"Of course you are."

Ava swallowed. "Guess this is goodbye."

"Yeah." He nodded once, slowly. "Guess so."

For a moment, neither moved.

It felt like a moment that should lead to something—a hug, a promise, a confession—but both of them stayed rooted to the ground.

Cole opened his mouth as if to say something else.

[Cole]: Tell her you'll see her. Tell her... something. Anything.

But a horn blared behind him, and his Uber rolled closer.

He stepped back. "I'll, uh... see you on Teams."

"Yeah. Teams." Her voice barely cooperated.

He gave her one last look—soft, warm, almost regretful—then climbed into the car.

Ava's Uber door opened, and she got in.

And as the car pulled away, her chest tightened with a truth she wouldn't let herself think about yet.

She didn't want that to be goodbye.
Not at all.

[Ava]: You are in so much trouble, Ava Harper.

CHAPTER FOUR

The Uber had barely pulled onto the freeway when Ava's phone buzzed. Again.

Brittany.

Ava sighed and answered. "Please tell me you're not crying into a seating chart."

"Oh, I passed that stage hours ago," Brittany wailed. "When will you be here? I'm hanging on by a thread. A literal thread, Aves."

"About twenty minutes," Ava said. "Deep breaths. Tell me what's happening."

"My mother," Brittany hissed, "is currently reorganizing the card box because she didn't like the energy.' Energy, Aves. Energy."

Ava winced sympathetically. "Okay, well my day was… also something."

[Ava]: Understatement of the century.

Brittany perked up instantly. "Tell me."

"Um. Well, I texted you my flight was canceled, right?"

"Annoying but standard."

"There was only one room left at the hotel they sent me to."

"Okay… slightly interesting."

"And I had to share it."

Silence.
Fatal silence.

[Ava]: Aaaand there it is.

"Aves," Brittany said slowly, "who did you share a room with?"

"My coworker, my male coworker," Ava muttered.

The shriek that followed nearly caused the Uber driver to swerve.

"You shared a room with a man you work with? How? Why was he there? Actually, we can unpack the details later. What is his name?."

Ava rubbed her forehead. "His name is Cole."

Brittany gasped. "Oh he has a hot name. He sounds hot."

"He's... normal," Ava lied, badly.

[Ava]: Tall, warm, devastatingly dimpled "normal." Sure.

"What does he look like?"

Ava hesitated. "Tall. Warm. Broad shoulders. Very... shirt-filling."

"Oh my God, you're into him," Brittany whispered. "I can hear it!"

"I am not—" Ava sputtered.

"You are! You described his shoulders. That's the first step toward emotional ruin."

Ava slumped in the seat. "We're coworkers, Britt. We'll never see each other in person again. We're literally heading in opposite directions."

[Ava]: Lies, lies, lies. But comforting, convenient lies.

"Fine," Brittany said dramatically. "But you owe me the full story the moment you get here."

The call ended shortly before the Uber slowed in front of Brittany and Zach's house.

Ava grabbed her suitcase, took one calming breath, and marched toward the porch.

[Ava]: Okay. No tripping. No falling. Just walk like a functioning adult for five seconds—

She made it up two steps before her toe caught the edge of the stair, and she pitched forward with the grace of a tranquilized flamingo.

A pair of strong hands caught her mid-fall.

"Whoa—easy."

47

She knew that voice.
She slowly looked up.

"Cole?" she yelped.

Cole Maddox blinked down at her, hands still gently bracing her arms. "Ava?"

[Cole]: Of course it's her. Of course the universe doubles down.

Before either of them could process anything, the front door flew open.

"Aves!" Brittany called, rushing out. "You made it! I need—"

She stopped dead.

Her eyes ping-ponged between Ava and the man holding her up.

Then she squealed. "Oh my God."

Zach appeared behind her, confused. "What's going—Maddox? Dude, why are you—"

He stopped too.

Ava looked between them, confused. "Wait. Why is Cole here?"

Zach snorted. Ava's eyes widened. She turned to Cole. "Why are you here?"

Cole awkwardly cleared his throat. "I'm the best man."

Ava's jaw dropped. "You're—Maddox? Zach's Maddox?"

Cole blinked at her. "Wait... wait. You're Aves? Brittany's Aves? She never shuts up about you."

[Cole]: Of course she's Aves. Of course, the girl you've been half in love with through a screen is one of your best friend's favorite people.

Brittany's gasp could've powered a small village. "Aves. You slept in the same room as Maddox?"

Ava slapped a hand over her face. "Can we not announce it to the neighborhood?"

Zach burst out laughing. "This is amazing."

[Ava]: This is chaos. Absolute chaos. And yet it feels... right? No. Don't think that you, idiot.

Brittany grabbed Ava's shoulders. "You two shared a bedroom."

"I slept on the couch," Cole said defensively.

"You still shared a space," Brittany squealed. "This is fate!"

"This is mortifying," Ava corrected.

[Ava]: Fate, mortification—same vibe.

Zach stepped aside, motioning toward the door. "Well, come on. You both live here for now. Best man suite upstairs, maid of honor room across the hall."

Ava blinked. "Wait—we're both staying here? The same house?"

"Uh, yeah?" Brittany said. "You're my maid of honor and house sitting next week. He's Zach's best man."

Ava slowly turned to Cole.

He gave her the softest, most sheepish smile.

"Surprise," he said gently.

[Cole]: Three days. Same house. No screen. You're dead, Cole.

Ava groaned.

"Oh," Brittany added, delighted, "this weekend is going to be so good."

Ava strongly suspected she meant "good" in a way that made her deeply, dangerously nervous.

Because despite every logical thought screaming at her.

Ava wasn't entirely sure she minded.

[Ava]: You're not surviving this weekend with your heart intact. Just accept it now.

Ava had barely escaped Brittany's interrogation when a knock sounded at the front door.

Brittany froze mid-rant. "Oh God. That's him."

"Who?" Ava asked.

Brittany winced. "Tony."

Ava's soul left her body.

[Ava]: This cannot be happening. Not right now. Not with Cole in the living room—

Zach jogged to the door and opened it.

Tony strutted in holding a cardboard box full of wedding stuff, wearing a polo shirt tucked into khakis with the confidence of a man who alphabetizes his spices by heat level.

"Ava!" he said brightly. "Hey! Mrs. Mills asked me to drop these off."

Ava forced a smile. "Hi, Tony."

[Ava]: Act normal. Act normal. Stop imagining Cole hearing every word—

Cole stood up from the couch slowly, arms

crossed over his chest, expression neutral in the way that was absolutely not neutral.

Tony set the box down and turned to Cole. "Oh, hey, I don't think we met. I'm Tony. Ava's wedding date."

Ava felt herself die inside.

Cole blinked once.
Then again.

Then slowly extended a hand. "Cole. I'm Ava's... coworker."

[Cole]: Do not crush his hand. Do not crush his hand. You cannot legally injure the man.

Tony gave a hearty, oblivious laugh, his gaze dropping to their suitcases "A coworker, huh? Very cool. So you guys traveled together?"

"No," Cole said instantly.

"Yes," Ava blurted at the same time.

They froze.

Brittany choked so loudly she nearly swallowed her tongue.

Tony raised an eyebrow. "Oh?"

Ava panicked. "Our connecting flight got canceled. We ended up at the same airport."

Cole cleared his throat. "And hotel."

Tony's head whipped toward him. "Hotel?"

Ava threw her hands up. "We had separate beds."

Cole nodded fast. "Separate beds."

Zach wheezed into his sleeve, trying not to laugh.

[Ava]: Fantastic. This is great. I love dying. Dying is my favorite.

Tony brightened. "Well, anyway. I should get going. See you at the wedding tomorrow."

Cole's jaw flexed.

Ava opened her mouth "I—um—yeah, at the wedding," she stammered.

Tony nodded, oblivious. "I'll text you."

The door closed behind him.
Silence.

Brittany immediately screamed into a throw pillow.

Zach muttered, "I am living for this drama."

Ava covered her face.
Cole rubbed the back of his neck.

[Cole]: Separate beds. Why did I say that like a confession?

"Okay!" Brittany announced, eyes bright with determination. "Now that *that* drama is done," she waved vaguely toward the door, "it's time to get ready to head to the rehearsal."

She pointed at Zach first. "Groom, you are not allowed to be late to your own rehearsal. I swear to God, if the planner beats us there again—"

Zach held up both hands. "I'm dressed. I'm ready. I've accepted my fate."

"Good," Brittany said. Then she turned to Ava. "Maid of honor, freshen up. Something cute but comfortable. And bring the vow cards. And maybe a tiny bit of emotional stability if you can find any."

Ava groaned. "No promises."

[Ava]: Perfect. Exactly the level of responsibility I'm capable of today.

"And you—" Brittany turned to Cole next, eyes narrowing like she was trying to read him through psychic bride powers. "Best man. Do you need five minutes to get ready, or are you one of those annoying men who's born prepared?"

Cole's mouth twitched. "I'm good."

"We'll see about that." She jabbed toward him.

"Tie on. Jacket steamed. Hair—" she circled her hand in the air at his head "—whatever situation this is—fixed."

Cole huffed out a quiet laugh but didn't argue.

[Cole]: She is terrifying. Respect.

Brittany clapped again. "Okay! Everyone has ten minutes. Ten. Then we're out the door. The bride and groom cannot—cannot—be late to their own rehearsal."

She stormed down the hall, muttering about schedules, candle arrangements, and how she would personally fight the planner if needed.

Zach followed her and resigned.

Ava headed upstairs toward her room, vow cards tucked under her arm.

Cole watched her for a second before falling in step behind her saying softly, "Need help with anything?" His vowels went soft and Southern in a way he absolutely didn't mean to let happen around her.

She shook her head quickly. "I've got it."

[Ava]: I do not "got it." Not even a little.

He nodded, though his eyes lingered a second longer than they should have.

[Cole]: Focus on the rehearsal. Please ignore the fact that she smells like vanilla and airport coffee.

Ava retreated into her guest room, closing the door behind her as her pulse ticked unhelpfully fast.

[Ava]: Okay. It's just a rehearsal. Just walking down an aisle with Cole. Very normal. Very fine. I'm totally not going to combust.

She changed quickly, touched up her makeup, grabbed her shoes and vow cards, and stepped back into the hallway that separated Cole's room from hers.

Cole emerged across the hall at the same moment, rolling his sleeves with a practiced ease. The crisp white shirt, dark slacks, and confident posture should've been illegal.

He paused when he saw her.

A heartbeat.
A flicker of something warm.

"You look nice," he said quietly.

Ava swallowed. "You too."

[Ava]: This is going to be a problem.

Brittany's voice echoed from downstairs: "Let's go people! We are already two minutes behind!"

Ava and Cole shared a look.

Then they headed down together—side by side—toward whatever fresh emotional disasters the rehearsal had waiting.

CHAPTER FIVE

The venue looked even more beautiful in person—vaulted pine beams, strings of soft lights, and an aisle lined with lanterns that glowed warm and golden.

Ava tightened her grip on her faux rehearsal bouquet.

[Ava]: Don't trip. Don't sweat. Don't pass out. Easy.

The planner—a petite woman with a headset and the energy of someone fueled entirely by caffeine and spreadsheets—clapped her hands.

"Okay, wedding party! Partners, find your match! Best man with maid of honor—Ava and Cole, that's you."

Ava froze.

Cole stepped up beside her with quiet confidence, offering his arm. "Ready?"

His voice was low and smooth—dangerously warm.

[Ava]: Left arm. Just take his left arm.

Ava nodded, trying not to stare at where his sleeve brushed her forearm.

She slipped her hand around his sleeve.

Cole inhaled sharply.

[Cole]: Focus. Walk. Don't pull her closer. Do not pull her closer.

The planner clapped once, briskly. "Okay! Cue music. Best man and maid of honor—walk."

Music filtered into the church, soft and echoing.

They stepped forward together.

Slow.
Steady.
Perfectly in sync.

Except Ava's brain had short-circuited entirely.

[Ava]: He smells good. Why is he allowed to smell this good? This is emotional warfare.

Cole fixed his eyes straight ahead, but his awareness kept straying sideways.

[Cole]: Ava in a soft blue dress, arm linked with mine. Fantastic. I'm absolutely doomed.

Behind them, the rest of the wedding party fell into line two by two, footsteps echoing down the center aisle. The sound layered over everything—fabric swishing, shoes quiet against wood floor, whisper-soft laughter as people settled into the rhythm.

Ava felt the room shift as they walked. Eyes followed them. Not openly—just little glances from pews, heads tilting, subtle double-takes.

She risked a quick look at Cole.
He was already looking at her.
Their eyes met—just a flicker.

Both snapped forward like they'd been caught doing something illegal.

A few steps later, it happened again.
This time, the look lingered.

A beat too long.

A smile curved at the corner of Cole's mouth before he could stop it. Ava fought the answering one that threatened to show.

[Ava]: Do not smile. People can see you.

From somewhere behind them, barely disguised whispers floated forward.

"They look good together."

"Like... really good."

"That energy? That's not rehearsal energy."

Ava pretended very intensely not to hear any of it.

[Ava]: This is basically a runway show of my emotional instability.

They reached the altar and separated—slowly.

Too slowly.

Cole's fingers skimmed free of her arm half a second later than necessary.

He noticed.
She noticed.

The entire collective group behind them absolutely noticed.

The planner, blissfully oblivious, clapped. "Lovely! Now let's do it again—but with smiles less... tight."

Ava blinked. "Tight?"

"You know," the planner said brightly. "Like you aren't fighting an intense internal battle."

Cole choked.

[Cole]: *She has no idea how accurate that is.*

They reset at the back of the aisle. Ava's heart thudded violently now.

Cole offered his arm again.

She hesitated for the smallest possible moment... then took it.

Their fingers brushed.
Both inhaled at the same time.

[Ava]: Nope. This is how people make catastrophic wedding decisions. Abort.

"Walking!" the planner called.

This pass, the looks came faster—less controlled. Ava's eyes drifted up to his face, caught on the softness there. Cole stole glances back, each one lingering a fraction longer than the last.

The gravity between them felt heavier now—palpable, like a current the room had started to sense. Conversations quieted. The wedding party behind them walked more slowly, unconsciously giving the pair too much space.

Halfway down, Ava's heel clipped the edge of Cole's shoe.

She stumbled.

Cole's hand flew to her waist, steadying her instinctively. Warmth pressed through the thin fabric.

[Cole]: Don't hold her. Don't lean in. Oh wow, she's soft—Absolutely do not think that.

"Got you," he murmured, a hint of a smile touching his mouth.

For a split second, they froze there—too close, breathing the same air—before she righted herself and stepped forward.

Just close enough that Ava felt the heat of him. Just long enough for the air between them to grow tight and fragile.

"Sorry," she breathed, scrambling back into position.

"You okay?" he said, his hand lingering another unavoidable second before dropping away.

Ava nodded. "Yeah."

Her pulse was absolutely lying to everyone about how *fine* she was.

They resumed the walk.

Slower now.
More careful.

Except something had shifted.

Ava could feel the way Cole looked at her—not just sideways this time, but openly, almost forgetting there were other people in the room. When she dared glance up again, his gaze was already waiting.

Not playful.
Not teasing.

Just... intent.

The kind of look that made the aisle feel

too short, and the space between them feel charged.

From a few steps behind, one of the bridesmaids leaned toward another, her whisper carrying farther than she meant it to.

"Did you see how he looks at her?"

A small pause.

"You don't look at someone like that for no reason."

Ava heard both.

Her skin went warm instantly. She fixed her eyes on the altar, pulse jumping.

[Ava]: They can see it.

They absolutely could see it.

Cole's jaw tightened as he caught the comment, his gaze snapping forward—but not before Ava felt the way his arm subtly *shifted closer to hers*, protective without even thinking about it.

They reached the altar again and separated.

This time, the space felt sharper.
Too wide.

As Brittany reached the altar on the final run of rehearsal, she clapped loudly, beaming.

"Yes! That. Do that exact thing tomorrow."

Ava wanted to dissolve physically.
Cole stared hard at the floor.

[Ava]: Tomorrow. As if I'm surviving tomorrow.

The planner checked her clipboard. "Perfect! That wraps rehearsal. Everyone, change if you need to, and head to the vineyard for dinner— we're on schedule. Barely."

The wedding party scattered, chatter rising immediately.

But Cole and Ava lingered, gravitating toward each other like it was the only movement that made sense.

Ava forced a tiny smile. "We did okay."

Cole returned it—but this time, there was something deeper resting in his eyes.

"We did..."

His voice fell lower at the end—soft, warm— a whisper of Louisiana slipping through enough to curl around the word.

Ava felt it buckle directly behind her knees.

He'd never sounded like that on their calls.

Not that warm.
Not that close.

"Ava Harper!"

The booming voice came from behind her, and before she could turn, arms wrapped around her and lifted her clean off the floor.

She yelped, laughing. "Nick, put me down!"

Nick grinned as he set her back on her feet. "I can't believe it. What's it been, two years?"

She punched him lightly in the arm. "I am not twelve anymore, and yet you still insist on picking me up every time you see me."

"Never stopping," he said cheerfully.

Cole stood a few steps away, watching the exchange. The familiarity hit first. The ease. The way Ava didn't flinch or hesitate just laughed, comfortable, known.

Something tight flickered in his chest. He shifted his weight forcing his expression neutral. He didn't love the way Nick's arm lingered around her shoulders or the way Ava leaned into the space like it belonged to her.

Before he could untangle whatever that reaction was supposed to mean, Zach clapped a hand on his shoulder.

"Hey, come here a sec," Zach said, already steering Cole toward a quiet corner of the venue.

Cole let himself be pulled away, casting one last glance back at Ava. She was still smiling, still laughing before Zach broke his attention away again.

"Quick questions. Possibly a big one." Zach said, clasping his hands together.

Cole glanced back toward Ava out of instinct. "Okay..."

"So," Zach said, rubbing his hands together. "You work remote, did you happen to bring your laptop with you?"

Cole paused, unsure of where this was going. "Uh. Yeah. Why?"

Zach let out a breath, relieved. "Well, I know you only planned to stay through Monday but, hypothetically, would you be able to stay for the week while Brittany and I are on our honeymoon?"

Cole blinked, confused. "Isn't Ava already house sitting?"

"Yeah, she is. Totally. Which is fine except Brittany is kind of spiraling."

He hesitated. "There's been a small uptick in break ins, and I told her it was fine. It's not even a neighborhood super close but she keeps saying she'd feel better if ava wasn't alone the whole week. I'm worried she's going to cancel the honeymoon or something, she gets impulsive when she spirals and..."

Zach's voice trailed off, the rest of his explanation dissolving into background noise as Cole thought about the idea.

[Cole]: A week in the same house means shared mornings, overlapping workdays, quiet evenings that didn't end with a call disconnecting or a screen going dark. Too much. Too close. But Ava wouldn't be alone and I can keep it professional... Right? Yeah.

He pictured Ava laughing in the kitchen. Barefoot. Comfortable. Real in way screens never allow.

The thought hit him low and warm and reckless.

[Cole]: No. I can't.

Zach cleared his throat. "So, uh... yeah. You would be doing me a huge solid."

Cole was pulled from his thoughts realizing the silence had stretched.

"Yeah," he said, the word slipping out before he could stop it.

Zach's face lit up. He pulled Cole into a quick, enthusiastic hug. "You're a lifesaver, man. Seriously. Thank you. I'll see you at the dinner..." he said as he walked away turning to give Brittany a thumbs up.

Cole turned back toward where Ava had been standing with Nick.

She was gone.

In her place stood a man about Cole's height, broad shouldered and effortlessly confident, with an easy grin and the kind of presence that filed the space without trying.

"Hey, man," Nick said, already closing the distance. "Cole, right? Ava said to tell you she'll see you at dinner. She got whisked away by my mom."

Of course she did.

[Cole]: Of course she did. Who is this guy?

"I'm Nick," he added extending his hand.

Cole took it and immediately felt his grip tighten, not aggressive. Just solid.

"Whoa," Nick laughed, releasing him. "Easy

there, dude. Just trying to shake your hand, not get my hand broken."

Then, like they were already friends, he jerked his thumb toward the door. "You can ride with me to dinner. I'm Ava's older brother by extension, apparently. Figured I should get to know you."

[Cole]: Oh. Why didn't I see it before? He looks just like Brittany. Now I feel like a dick.

"Sorry man—for the gorilla grip."

Nick laughed. "All good." As they headed towards the exit together.

CHAPTER SIX

The house fell into a soft, exhausted quiet after the rehearsal dinner. Ava slipped upstairs and down the hallway toward her room, heels dangling from one hand, trying not to replay every ridiculous, heart-racing moment of the night.

Walking with Cole during rehearsal.
The looks across the dinner table.

The way he'd almost touched her carelessly and instinctively more times than either of them admitted.

[Ava]: The lingering brush of his hand at the small of your back? That was nothing. Totally nothing. Ignore how your brain replays it every six seconds.

Her brain was a traitor.

As soon as she shut her bedroom door, Ava let her head fall back against it.

"Okay," she whispered. "Dress off. Pajamas on. Avoid Cole Maddox for the next twelve hours."

She reached for her zipper.

It didn't budge.
She tugged harder.

Still nothing.

"Oh no. No. No—" she muttered, contorting herself into a sad, wiggling pretzel. "Come on, you evil, overpriced satin death trap—"

She yanked.
The zipper refused.

And then her hand slipped.
Thunk.

"Ow!" Ava hissed, rubbing her elbow.

A pause.

Then—A soft knock.

"Ava...?" Cole's voice, warm and ridiculously close through the door. "You okay?"

[Ava]: Of course, he heard you losing a fight with fabric.

Ava froze, mid-contortion. "I—yes. No! I mean—I'm fine. Totally fine. Just fighting with my zipper."

A breathy laugh came from the other side. "Do you want help?"

"No," she blurted.

Then, quieter: "...maybe."

A longer pause.
Weighted.
Alive.

[Cole]: This is a bad idea. Don't go in. Don't touch her. Don't—

"Can I come in?" he asked gently.

Ava cracked the door open just enough to peek out. He stood barefoot in joggers and a white T-shirt that fit too well, hair slightly messy like he'd raked his fingers through it.

[Ava]: Fantastic. He's in "boyfriend dropping by" clothes, not "coworker" clothes. Great. Perfect.

She opened the door fully.

He stepped in slowly—carefully—like one wrong move might set the room on fire. Honestly, it might.

She turned, revealing the stubborn zipper, reaching back to gather her hair and sweep it over one shoulder. Most of it moved obediently—but a few loose strands slipped free, clinging to the curve of her neck and brushing the edge of her shoulder blade.

His breath caught.
Barely.

But enough.

[Cole]: Do not think about how warm her skin is. You're just fixing a zipper. That's it. Nothing else... right. Sure.

She stilled, waiting.

His fingers lifted—slow, deliberate—as he brushed the stray strands aside. His fingertips skimmed the slope of her neck, followed the line of her shoulder just enough to guide the hair away.

Gentle.
Curious.

Heat bloomed wherever he touched her.
A spark shot straight down her spine.

His fingers lingered at the base of her neck for a suspended heartbeat longer than necessary.

Her shoulders softened without her even realizing it. She settled—just the faintest bit—into the quiet steadiness of him standing there.

[Ava]: Okay. Yep. That's it. I'm actually going to combust.

"Okay," he said low, his voice smooth with that slow, easy lilt that warmed her soul. "It's just caught on the fabric."

One hand found the zipper. The other brushed the fabric at her back—hovering, then settling briefly at her waist, warm and anchoring.

Not holding her.
Just... there.

He worked the zipper free with controlled patience.

Then—

The zipper slid down with a soft, traitorous sigh.

Ava's breath stuttered. Her chest tightened, suddenly too full of nerves and desire and awareness she wasn't ready for.

"Thanks," she whispered, barely turning to steal a glance at him.

He didn't move.
Didn't remove his hand.

The space between them narrowed as they both leaned—slightly, slowly—toward each other. She could feel the whisper of his breath in her hair, the lingering warmth of his palm at her back.

Warm.
Careful.
Devastating.

More intention than movement—but it felt like a confession all the same.

He felt it. She knew he did.

[Cole]: Step back, Cole. You want her too much. And wanting her this much feels dangerous, like one wrong breath might fracture the fragile line you're balancing on.

But he didn't step back.

He stayed, caught between instinct and restraint, every second stretching taut between them.

Until—

"Aves?! I need lipstick advice." Brittany's voice rang from the living room.

Ava jumped, breath catching in her throat. Cole lurched backward like the sound physically pulled him away, hitting the dresser with a muted thud.

For a long heartbeat, they stared—both flushed, both shaken, both caught in the gravity of what they almost let happen.

He swallowed hard. "I-uh—should go," he said softly, the roughness in his voice betraying everything he wasn't saying. "Goodnight."

He hesitated in the doorway—one last, aching moment—before he forced himself to leave.

[Cole]: Run. Before you turn around and kiss her like an idiot.

"Goodnight," she managed.

He slipped out the door, closing it gently behind him.

Ava stood frozen, staring at the space, the air still warm from where he'd been.

"Oh no," she whispered. "Not okay."

Her pulse fluttered painfully.
She wanted that. Too much.

And then, the quieter truth.

[Ava]: You can't do long distance again. You can't want someone who doesn't live in your world, in your city, in your everyday.

But the ache in her chest didn't care about logistics or time zones or three-hour flights. It cared about the way he looked at her like she was something he couldn't walk away from— even when he just did.

Ava pressed her palms to her face, breath shivering out of her.

"This is... bad," she whispered into her hands. "This is really, really bad."

She peeled off the dress with a sigh of relief, swapping it for soft, patterned sleep pants, a simple tank, and the cardigan she always traveled with. After splashing cold water on her face until the blush settled, she headed into the hallway, down the stairs and straight to Brittany.

Brittany was in the living room, waving a makeup bag. "Lipstick! Now!"

Ava sat on the edge of the couch while Brittany held up two shades like they were weapons.

But Brittany froze mid-sentence.
Her eyes narrowed.
Slowly, dramatically, she leaned closer.

"Aves... why are you pink?"

"I'm not."

"You are very pink."

"I'm fine."

Brittany gasped like she'd uncovered a government secret. "It is because of Maddox, isn't it?"

"Britt—"

"Oh my God, I knew it. What happened?"

"My zipper was stuck. He helped me unzip my dress."

Brittany screamed into a pillow. "I knew it!"

"It wasn't like that!"

"Did he see your bra?"

"Brittany!"

Brittany fanned herself. "Seriously. This *is* better than reality TV."

[Ava]: Unfortunately, it's my actual life.

Ava groaned. "Can we please pick a lipstick?"

They chose a soft rose shade after an entire dissertation of analysis, and Brittany finally released her with a knowing smirk.

Ava grabbed a glass of water from the kitchen before heading back upstairs, down the dark hallway toward her room.

She turned the corner and walked straight into warm, unyielding muscle.

Water splashed everywhere.

"Oh my God—sorry—I—"

Cole's hands found her.

Not by accident.
Not reflex.
He chose to.

One hand slid to her waist; the other braced against the wall beside her head, guiding her back until her spine met the wall.

Slow.
Intentional.
Devastating.

Her breath faltered.

His chest rose and fell against hers—too close, too real, impossible to ignore.

His damp shirt clung to him, outlining every unfair inch of him.

[Ava]: A+ timing to notice details, Ava. Truly.

"Aves..." he breathed, voice low and warm enough to melt her bones.

[Ava]: Was that new—Aves? Or had he always called me that? Britt and Zach used it all the time but hearing it from him? I might actually melt.

Her fingers tightened in his shirt—instinct, panic, longing tangled together.

He leaned in.
Closer.
Closer still.

Their foreheads brushed. Then their noses.

Her lips parted without permission, despite every sensible thought telling her not to.

[Ava]: *Don't want this. Don't want him.*

A lie.

[Ava]: *Because if you want him, you could lose him. Because long distance never works for you. Because wanting someone you can't keep always ends the same way.*

But her heart didn't care about any of it.
Not tonight.

She tilted up that final inch.

Their lips grazed—barely there, barely touching—but enough to send heat rushing through her like her nerves had been waiting for this moment.

Her hand shook—just enough for the empty glass to slip from her fingers.

It hit the hardwood with a loud clink—clatter—roll.

Cole jolted like reality had slapped him across the face.

He stepped back fast, eyes wide, chest heaving, hands lifted like his body had hit pause.

"Cole..." she breathed.

He shook his head—hard.

As if trying to break whatever spell had wrapped around them.

"You're my coworker," he said, voice cracking. "I can't—Ava, I just..."

[Cole]: You're not supposed to want this. Not with her. Not like this. Not when your entire life is tied up with hers at work.

He didn't finish.
Didn't need to.

He stepped back again.
Then again.

Putting distance between them like it physically hurt. "I'm sorry," he whispered.

Her heart squeezed. "You didn't... do anything wrong."

[Ava]: We both did. And it felt way too right.

His eyes flicked to her lips one last time.

[Cole]: Stop. God, stop before you ruin everything again.

The heat between them snapped into something sharper, memory slamming into him with sickening clarity—the whispers, the fallout, the way Bree walked out of that job because being near him had become too heavy, too complicated, too painful.

[Cole]: Don't do that to her. Don't drag her into another one of your messes because you can't control yourself.

Another flash—his old coworker's face, the last time he saw her.

The quiet hurt.
The resignation.

The way he'd stood there, feeling like he'd broken something he couldn't fix.

[Cole]: Not again. Not her.

What happened with Bree had been painful, yes. Messy. Full of guilt, he still carried. But it hadn't been this.

Ava was more.

So much more, he didn't have a word for it yet. If he ruined her life the way he'd ruined Bree's? He'd never recover.

His breath stalled. He tore his gaze from her mouth like the air between them burned.

It ruined him.

He turned quickly before he could change his mind, walking down the hall with stiff, tormented steps.

Ava stayed pressed to the wall, chest rising and falling, water cooling on her skin.

Her fingers touched her lips.

They still tingled.

"Yeah," she whispered into the quiet house. "I'm completely screwed."

CHAPTER SEVEN

Ava groaned into her pillow as her alarm beeped—set far earlier than she ever woke up on purpose. But it was the wedding day, and Brittany needed her.

Fantastic. Perfect. Exactly how she wanted to start a morning while pretending the hallway with Cole wasn't still buzzing under her skin.

She dragged herself to the backyard, where Brittany sat curled in a blanket, two mugs already waiting—the early morning light filtered over the fence, soft and warm.

"You okay?" Ava asked, taking the mug, as Brittany slid toward her.

Brittany exhaled. "Trying to take it in. Before everything gets loud."

Ava sat beside her. "You're allowed to be overwhelmed. It's your wedding day."

Brittany shot her a sideways look. "And *you* seem... extremely preoccupied."

Ava nearly choked on her coffee. "I'm fine."

"You're lying."

"Obviously."

Brittany grinned. "It's Maddox, isn't it?"

Ava groaned into her mug. "Please don't do this to me before eight a.m."

"So something *did* happen," Brittany whispered, eyes lighting up. "Bless you for giving me a distraction before I start crying again."

Ava covered her face. "It wasn't a thing. It was barely anything."

Brittany leaned closer. "But it was something."

Ava didn't answer.
She didn't need to.

Her silence was its own confession.

Brittany squeezed her arm, softer now. "Whatever it was... you're allowed to feel it, Aves."

Ava swallowed hard. "Can we not unpack my entire emotional crisis on your wedding morning?"

Brittany laughed. "Fine. For now."

She suddenly jolted upright, adrenaline sparking. "Okay, we need to get moving. Hair and makeup arrive in fifteen."

Ava blinked. "fifteen minutes?!"

"Welcome to the wedding day!" Brittany called, already rushing inside.

Ava followed, bracing herself.

The makeup artist and hair stylist arrived with rolling cases and ring lights, transforming the dining room into a glam battlefield—palettes, curling irons, fake lashes—organized chaos everywhere.

Ava sat beside Brittany as the stylists got to work.

As a brush swept across Ava's cheek, Brittany nudged her gently. "Just checking... still not talking about last night?"

Ava narrowed her eyes. "Not unless you want me to cry and ruin this woman's excellent contouring."

Brittany grinned. "Fair."

They shared a look—fond, chaotic, sister-deep—and then let the room buzz around them.

Meanwhile, upstairs, Zach stood in the guest room designated for the groomsmen, adjusting his shirt, while Cole frowned at a tie that absolutely didn't need adjusting.

"You good?" Zach asked.

Cole's jaw flexed. "Yep."

"That's a lie," Zach replied instantly.

Cole huffed. "Obviously."

Zach smirked. "You gonna tell me why you look like you wrestled with your conscience all night?"

Cole didn't answer.
Which was an answer.

Zach clapped him on the shoulder. "Whatever it is, deal with it tomorrow. Today's about Brittany."

Cole nodded, but his eyes drifted toward the sounds downstairs—distant laughter, clinking glasses, and the unmistakable sound of Ava's voice.

Zach noticed. He smirked again. "Right. Definitely tomorrow."

By the time Ava and Brittany reentered the living room, the house had transitioned from peaceful morning to full-blown wedding machine: hairpins, garment bags, champagne flutes, and distant shouts about missing earrings.

Perfect, joyful chaos.
And also—Tony.

Tony arrived fumbling with the handles of a too-bright gift bag, beaming like an emotional support Labrador at a dog park.

"Ava! Morning! You look great."

Ava smiled tightly. "Hi, Tony."

[Ava]: He's kind. He's harmless. He's also about as interesting to you romantically as a damp sock.

Brittany shot Ava a sympathetic grimace over Tony's shoulder. "Sorry," she mouthed.

Ava shrugged back. She'd survive.

Cole appeared at the bottom of the stairs, adjusting his tie and looking like a walking heart complication. Their eyes met.

A beat.
A hiccup in the universe.

He looked away first—quick, almost guilty—like the sight of her cost him something.

[Cole]: Professional. Right. We're being professional today. Good.

"Maddox!" Zach hollered from the kitchen. "Your date's almost here."

Cole froze. He had forgotten. Zach set him up with a girl from the local coffee shop.

Then the doorbell rang.

A blonde woman stepped inside wearing a tight champagne-colored dress, heels too tall for common sense, lipstick too red for daylight. She surveyed the room like she was auditioning for a perfume commercial.

"Maddox?" she purred.

He stepped forward. "Uh—hi. You must be Carly."

Ava tried not to stare.
She failed.

Carly wrapped her arms around Cole's neck. Ava's teeth pressed together before she could stop it, tension shooting into her jaw like a reflex she didn't ask for.

"A pleasure," Carly drawled.

Cole's hands hovered awkwardly in the air, barely touching her back.

[Ava]: Abort mission. Nope. Absolutely not the vibe.

Ava looked away, cheeks burning for reasons she didn't want to examine.

Tony stepped closer. "I brought snacks for the limo ride."

Ava smiled politely.

[Ava]: Please stop being so innocent and friendly. I'm too emotionally compromised to handle it.

Brittany clapped. "Limo loading in ten minutes. Let's go, bridal squad."

The drive to the venue was a haze of chatter. Carly spent most of it explaining to Cole her plans for a boutique dog bakery business ("Pupcakes."), while Cole stared out the window like he was calculating escape routes.

Meanwhile, Tony told Ava about his job in wealth management. In detail. Painfully thorough detail.

Ava nodded politely while her brain imagined the sweet release of passing out.

[Ava]: Okay, universe. I get it. Punish me for almost definitely kissing my coworker. Very funny.

The ceremony setup was stunning—lakeside view, floating floral arch, rows of chairs filled with guests.

Ava adjusted Brittany's train, heart pounding for reasons unrelated to wedding nerves.

Cole stood across the aisle with the groomsmen, looking everywhere except at Ava.

[Ava]: Good. We're on the same page— avoidance: activated.

The planner called out, "Okay! Best man and maid of honor—time to line up."

Ava took her place.

Cole approached from the opposite end of the aisle. They met in the middle.

For a single moment, the whole venue narrowed down to his hand offering his arm to her.

"Ready?" he murmured.

His voice was soft.
Too soft.

Ava nodded. "Yeah."

[Ava]: No, you're not. You're absolutely not.

When their arms linked, his warmth hit her like a memory she wasn't prepared for.

He swallowed.

[Cole]: Don't look at her. Don't remember last night. Don't want this more than you should.

The music started.
They walked.

Slow.
Steady.
Together.

Guests watched. Cameras flashed. Bridesmaids whispered.

Tony grinned from the third row like this was a rom-com he wanted front-row seats to.

Carly waved at Cole from her seat with the enthusiasm of a Price is Right contestant.

Ava kept her eyes forward.
Cole kept his jaw tight.

[Ava]: Focus. Keep your heart from falling out of your chest.

The ceremony went perfectly—vows, laughter, and tears.

Ava held Brittany's bouquet during the kiss. Cole passed the rings smoothly. They stood together in photos, smiling stiffly.

They didn't speak beyond necessary whispers.

[Ava]: Distance. Good. Safe. Logical.

The reception was held at a vineyard glowing with fairy lights strung through towering oak trees. It was warm, fragrant, golden—the kind of place where magic was embarrassingly easy.

The bridal party sat at a long table facing the dance floor. Tony sat beside Ava, blissfully friendly. Cole sat stiffly, shoulders locked, as Carly draped herself over him like a decorative scarf. He shot Ava a quick, helpless glance—one she pretended not to see.

Carly snapped a selfie. "Smile, babe!"

Cole offered a weak half-smile.

[Ava]: I hate this. Why does this bother me? It shouldn't. It really shouldn't.

Something in Ava's chest pinched—sharp, stupid, and absolutely uninvited.

Tony leaned over. "You okay, Ava?"

"Hm? Totally fine. I love being fine. It's my full-time hobby."

[Ava]: You're so not fine. You're a cracked vase with glitter glue holding you together.

Dinner passed. Toasts were made. Tony talked about investing. Carly talked loudly about her exes. Ava drank more wine than she intended. Cole sipped his slowly like he was trying not to lose control.

Then the DJ called everyone to the dance floor for the wedding party dance.

Brittany leaned over the table to Ava. "Time to break the tension."

Ava blinked. "What?"

Across the table, Zach whispered something to Cole. Cole looked up sharply at him.

Then at Ava. Then back at Zach with an expression that said *absolutely not*.

Zach grinned like a gremlin.

The DJ spoke into the mic. "Maid of honor and best man—Ava and Cole—join the couple on the dance floor."

Ava's stomach dropped.

Cole stood.
She stood.

They approached each other under the lights.

He extended his hand.
She took it.

Warm.
Steady.
Dangerous.

Cole swallowed hard. "Ava, we don't... have to make this weird." The last word wavered, his vowels softening in that way they did when he was slipping—tipsy, nervous, too honest.

Ava felt her breath catch.

He didn't even realize he was doing it, how the faint drawl thickened when he stopped overthinking.

[Ava]: Everything is already weird. This whole weekend has been strange. I'm in love with weird.

She stepped closer as the music started.
They swayed.

Slow.
Close.

Ava kept her eyes on his chest because looking up would unravel her. Cole kept his hand respectfully at her waist, fingers trembling the slightest bit.

Carly watched from her table, arms crossed, clearly irritated.

Tony looked confused but cheerful.

Brittany beamed.
Zach winked.

Cole's breath brushed Ava's temple.

"Aves..." he murmured, barely audible. Her name rolled out of him slow and unguarded, the softest Louisiana heat threading through.

It wasn't just her name—It was a weakness.

Or maybe it was hers. Because the sound of it nearly unraveled her right there in his arms.

Her heart stuttered.

"Yes?"

He hesitated.
Closed his eyes.
Then shook his head.

"Nothing."

[Cole]: Everything.

The song ended, but Cole didn't drop her hand immediately.

Neither moved.

"Aves," Brittany hissed loudly from behind them, "Cake time!"

Ava jumped back like she'd been yanked from a dream.

"Right! Cake! Important cake things."

She fled.

Cole pressed a hand to the back of his neck.

[Cole]: Get it together. You're losing your damn mind.

The reception had thinned, guests drifting toward shuttles or lingering near the dance floor. Fairy lights glimmered above the vineyard patio as Ava helped Brittany gather her bouquet.

That was when Brittany's expression shifted.

Her smile went slow. Sharp.

"Aves," she said lightly, "quick question."

Ava narrowed her eyes. "No."

Brittany laughed. "You don't even know what I'm asking."

"I know your face," Ava said. "That's a *plotting* face."

Zach appeared at Brittany's side, arm looping easily around her waist. He looked... guilty.

Brittany tilted her head. "So—you know you're house-sitting for us all week."

"Yes," Ava said carefully. "That part I agreed to."

"Great," Brittany said. "Because we made one tiny adjustment."

Ava froze. "Brittany."

"We just didn't want you alone," Brittany continued, too smoothly. "And since Maddox already works remote—"

"No," Ava said. "Absolutely not."

Zach winced. "Maybe let her finish?"

Ava pointed at Brittany. "You are matchmaking. I don't need match making."

"I am *protecting*," Brittany corrected. "From loneliness. And possibly burglars."

"There are no burglars," Ava hissed.

"There was a *tiny spike*," Zach offered weakly.

Ava ignored him. "You already planned this!"

Brittany smiled, unapologetic. "Yes."

Ava stared at her. "You're enjoying this, aren't you?"

"Immensely."

Before Ava could launch into a full protest, Zach lifted a hand and waved someone over.

Cole turned from the dance floor, tie loosened, sleeves rolled, hair a little too charmingly undone. He approached cautiously, as if he already suspected he was being summoned into danger.

"What's going on?" he asked.

Ava crossed her arms. "Apparently, you're moving in with me."

Cole blinked.
Once.

Then again.

He looked at Zach. "You didn't talk to Ava before you talked to me?"

Before Zach could answer, Brittany slid in smoothly.

"I was going to," she said. "But you said yes so fast it felt... unnecessary."

Ava whipped toward her. "You asked him *first*?"

Brittany smiled, unapologetic. "Of course I did. Well, Zach did."

Cole shifted, leaning toward Ava. "I thought you knew," he said quietly.

Zach held up his hands. "In my defense, Brittany was spiraling, I couldn't let my beautiful bride spiral."

"Excuse me," Ava said, poking him in the chest, "but you could have talked to both of us at the same time, Zach."

Brittany leaned in, delighted. "But you're not saying no now."

Ava glared at her. "You are scheming."

"I am ensuring emotional support and home security," Brittany countered. "Very different."

Cole cleared his throat. "If it helps—I haven't changed my flight yet. I don't have to stay if you don't want—"

"You already said yes," Ava cut in.

Her pulse betrayed her instantly.

He nodded once. "Yeah."

She opened her mouth—to protest, to argue, to reclaim some sense of control—

"I can stay with—"

Nick's voice cut in as he approached.

Brittany whipped around, her smile vanishing. She lifted one finger and drew it across her throat in a silent, unmistakable warning.

Nick stopped mid-step, mouth snapping shut. He lifted his hands in surrender.

"I was just offering—"

"Noted," Brittany said sweetly. "And rejected."

Ava pressed her lips together, fighting a laugh.

Ava pressed her lips together, fighting a laugh. Nick backed away, disappearing into the small crowd that was left on the dance floor.

Brittany clapped her hands and turned back

to Zach. "We should probably start our goodbyes and thank-yous, with the evening wrapping up."

And suddenly, it was just Ava and Cole.

The space between them felt louder without everyone else filling it.

"So," Ava said softly. "Guess we're... roommates."

Cole smiled, small and crooked. "Guess so."

He stepped forward.

Just enough to close the narrow space between them.

Ava didn't move back.
Didn't move forward.

The air between them went tight.
Charged.

Too close to pretend this was nothing.

His gaze dipped, tracking the line of her face—lingering somewhere he very deliberately didn't act on.

"Hey," he murmured.

Then he leaned in—not down far enough for a kiss, not back enough to retreat—and slid one arm around her shoulders, pulling her in.

It wasn't quite a hug. More like he'd meant to hold her and stopped halfway through the decision.

Her cheek pressed fully to his chest. His hand rested at her upper back, firm for half a second—long enough to feel like a choice—before it stilled. The solid warmth of him grounding and overwhelming all at once.

His body didn't relax.
Neither did hers.
It lasted a beat too long to be friendly.

Then he stepped back abruptly, clearing his throat, hands dropping to his sides like he'd physically pried them away from her.

"Sorry," he said quietly. "That was—" He stopped, shook his head. "Felt like the safest option."

Ava swallowed, her skin still warm where he'd touched her.

"Yeah," she said. "Very... safe."

Their eyes met again.

The distance between them felt larger now. And somehow, worse.

[Ava]: Oh no. This week is absolutely going to ruin me.

CHAPTER EIGHT

By the time they pulled into Brittany and Zach's driveway, it was just a little past 10:30 p.m. A little early for a wedding night, but Zach had insisted the reception wrap before everyone turned into pumpkin-slumped zombies.

Inside, the house glowed with warm lamplight. Brittany kicked off her heels in the foyer with a groan of pure relief.

"Why," she announced, "did I think getting married in heels was a good idea?"

Zach laughed, loosening his tie as he headed into the kitchen. "Babe, you wore them for thirty minutes."

"That is thirty minutes too long," she snapped dramatically, then dropped onto the sofa like a marionette with its strings cut.

Ava smiled, warmth pooling in her chest. This was the version of Brittany she loved the most—dramatic, exhausted, happy beyond words.

Cole set the gift bags down near the dining table, then paused awkwardly, unsure where to place himself now that the wedding fog had lifted.

Brittany pointed at him. "Sit."

Cole blinked. "Uh—okay?"

"Sit and tell me how beautiful I was," she demanded.

Zach returned from the kitchen with four glasses of water. "You were gorgeous, babe."

"See?" she said, waving toward him. "Supportive husband energy. Maddox, match it."

Cole sat on the chair beside the couch, rubbing the back of his neck. "You were beautiful, Brittany."

"Thank you," she said smugly, then jabbed a finger toward Ava. "And you were stunning. My most perfect, loyal, organized little maid of honor."

Ava rolled her eyes but smiled. "Love you too, dramatic gremlin."

Brittany yawned. "Okay, wedding recap. Hit me. What was your favorite part?"

Ava laughed. "The vows."

Zach said, "The champagne tower."

Cole said, "When Zach tripped over a lantern and pretended he meant to."

Zach groaned. "I knew you saw that."

They all laughed, the easy glow of the night still lingering.

For a moment, everything felt simple.

Warm.
Normal.

Then Brittany sat up straighter, blinking blearily. "Okay—we have three hours to pack before bed."

"Babe," Zach sighed. "Can't we do this tomorrow morning?"

"No," she said firmly. "Because tomorrow morning I will be useless and full of airport rage."

Ava stood. "For the record, I fully support pre-rage planning."

Cole smothered a smile behind his glass of water.

Brittany pushed up from the sofa and groaned again. "Alright, you two," she said, pointing vaguely between Ava and Cole, "go relax or whatever. We'll pack, sleep a little, and leave you in charge of the whole house tomorrow."

Ava's stomach fluttered. "Right. House-sitting."

Cole nodded subtly beside her without looking her way.

Zach clapped Cole on the shoulder. "Make yourself at home, Maddox. Towels are out back if you want to sit by the pool."

"And don't break anything," Brittany called as they disappeared down the hallway.

"Or have sex on our couch!" Zach added, voice echoing. Ava choked on her own breath. "Zach!"

Brittany cackled. "Ignore him!"

The bedroom door shut behind them, leaving the house abruptly quiet.

Ava and Cole stood there a moment.

Just breathing.
Just listening to the silence.
Just aware.

Ava cleared her throat. "I—uh—I'm going to change. I can't do another minute in this dress."

Cole's gaze flicked over her for half a second before he caught himself. His hands slid into his pockets, shoulders tightening like he needed somewhere to put all that sudden energy.

"Yeah," he said softly. "Take your time."

There was something in his voice—low, careful, a little too gentle—that made her pulse jump.

Ava slipped upstairs. Changing into soft shorts and a worn-in T-shirt took less than a minute, but calming the flutter under her ribs took longer.

When she came back down, Cole was still exactly where she'd left him, like he hadn't let himself move. His posture straightened the instant he saw her.

They shared a small, charged smile.

Ava shoved her hands into her shorts pockets to hide how unsteady they felt. "Want to sit outside? I feel like I haven't had a second to breathe."

"Yeah," he said again—quieter this time, as if the word meant more than it should.

Outside, the night was soft and warm, the pool glowing with deep turquoise light. The string lights overhead flickered faintly, casting everything in a hazy, romantic glow.

Ava sank onto a lounge chair, pulling her knees up. Her oversized T-shirt slid just slightly off her shoulder.

She didn't pull it back up.

Cole sat beside her, stretching his long legs out, rolling his sleeves with slow, deliberate care—movement so restrained it felt like its own kind of confession.

They didn't talk at first.
They just... existed.

Together.
Finally, Ava asked softly, "How are you feeling? After today?"

Cole let out a long breath. "Good. Tired. Overstimulated. Grateful Zach didn't actually trip a second time."

Ava laughed. "It was touch-and-go during the speeches."

He smiled.

Then his expression shifted. Softer. More vulnerable.

"And you?" he asked quietly.

She didn't lie.

"Confused," Ava said. "A little overwhelmed. A little... excited."

His brows pulled together. "Excited?"

She hesitated.

Then nodded.

"Yeah."

He looked away, pulse jumping in his throat.

[Cole]: Don't mess this up. Don't say the wrong thing. Don't let her see how much that one word hit you.

Ava pulled the blanket across her lap. "I meant... about the next few days. House-sitting. Time to relax. To breathe."

She swallowed.
[Ava]: To be near you.

She didn't say it.
She didn't have to.

Cole nodded once. "Yeah. Me too."

And then—like someone loosened a knot—the conversation flowed.

About their childhood summers.

Favorite movies.
Worst bosses.
Travel horror stories.

The moment Ava admitted she once walked into the wrong meeting and sat through an hour-long budget review because she was too embarrassed to leave, Cole nearly spilled his drink laughing.

And when Cole confessed he gets motion sick on boats despite his family being heavily involved in fishing, Ava laughed so hard she snorted.

Time blurred.

The backyard world felt small and warm and safe.

Ava pulled her legs onto the chair and wrapped her blanket around her shoulders. Cole shifted closer so they were angled toward each other—not touching, but close enough to feel the warmth between them.

Midnight slipped past.
Then one.
Then nearly two.

Finally, Ava whispered, "We should probably sleep. They're leaving early."

Cole nodded, though he didn't stand. "Yeah."

Ava hesitated. "Tonight was... nice."

He smiled.

Slow.
Small.
True.

"It was."

Ava stood, gathering her blanket and turning toward the house. She needed distance before she said something she couldn't take back.

She didn't make it a whole step.

Cole rose with her—deliberately—and his hand came to her arm. Not brushing. Not accidental. A quiet, intentional touch that asked her to stay.

Ava stilled.

He closed the distance slowly, decisively, as if some internal debate had finally ended. His hand shifted to her side, guiding her back toward him—not claiming, just certain.

Ava let herself lean into that certainty. The contact grounded her, eased something she hadn't realized she'd been holding.

His breath lingered at her temple. Before he could talk himself out of it, he dipped his head and kissed her cheek—soft, careful, like he was afraid of breaking something fragile.

Ava's inhale caught.

Then low and unguarded, "Being around you..." he murmured, "has never been the kind of simple I pretend it is. Even on video calls."

The words weren't a confession. Just truth, he'd stopped bothering to hide.

Ava didn't answer.
She didn't need to.

She stayed where she was, letting the moment exist—warm, terrifying, right.

Cole exhaled softly against her hair before easing back enough to meet her eyes.

"Goodnight, Aves."

Ava swallowed, pulse still fluttering. "Goodnight, Cole."

She stepped inside before she did something neither of them could walk back from.

CHAPTER NINE

Ava wasn't sure what woke her.

The soft thump of a suitcase rolling down the hall? Brittany whisper-screaming at Zach? The front door opening and closing twice in a row?

No—it was the knock.

"Aves!" Brittany whisper-yelled through the guest room door. "We're leaving! Love you! Keep our house alive."

Ava groaned into her pillow. "Goodbye. Please don't die."

"We'll try!" Brittany chirped. "Also—don't do anything I wouldn't do."

Zach's voice echoed faintly, "That covers like... three things, babe."

"Shh!"

Ava heard kissing noises, shuffling, the sound of keys dropping, picking up again, and then finally—finally—blessed silence.

She exhaled.

[Ava]: They're gone. We're alone. Holy shit.

Footsteps padded down the hall.
A soft knock.

Then Cole's voice, warm and unfairly awake.

"Ava? They just left. No rush, but... do you want coffee?"

Ava pulled the blanket over her face.

Her brain replayed the moment he'd pulled her against him the night before. Bad. Very bad. Too early in the morning to feel that much.

She forced herself to sound marginally human. "Mmm... yes."

"Okay," Cole said gently. "I'll put a mug out for you."

The footsteps faded.
Ava flopped onto her back.

[Ava]: Why is he a morning person? Why.

She dragged herself out of bed, hair a mess, T-shirt twisted, sleep lines on her cheek. She splashed water on her face, brushed her teeth, threw on leggings and a sweatshirt, and silently prayed she didn't look like a crime scene.

Then she made her way downstairs.

Cole was in the kitchen, barefoot, hair still damp from his shower, wearing a fitted T-shirt that made her stop—her attention catching on the strong lines of his back, the way muscle shifted beneath the fabric when he moved.

He looked over his shoulder. He froze for a breath—a barely-there flicker of last night in his expression—before he recovered.

"Morning," he said, voice softer now.

Ava blinked at him. "...How are you alive right now?"

He laughed under his breath. "I'm always up early."

"Why."

"Habit."

"No." Ava's mouth tipped into a faint smile.

"No?" he echoed, amused.

He slid a coffee mug toward her—her favorite color, somehow—along with a spoon and a small bowl of sugar.

"I didn't know how you take it," he said.

Her heart did something stupid and warm.

Uncomfortable.
Nice.

She swallowed. "Thanks."

He nodded once, turning back to the counter.

Ava took her first sip of coffee, nearly moaned, and then remembered Cole Maddox was standing three feet away.

She set the mug down like it might explode.

Cole smirked without looking. "Good?"

"Shut up."

He chuckled.

[Ava]: Okay. No. He isn't allowed to be this attractive in the morning. That should be a crime punishable by fines.

Ava leaned against the counter. "So... we have a whole day ahead of us."

Cole nodded, pulling his laptop from his bag. "Yeah. Probably good to get a few things sorted before we're back to work on Wednesday."

"Agreed."

They stood in comfortable silence for a moment.

Then Ava said, "So. What's first?"

"Laundry."

Ava smiled, amused. "I planned ahead. I'm fine."

Cole let out a small, sheepish laugh. "Yeah, I didn't."

He nodded toward the hallway. "If you end up needing anything washed, you can throw it in with mine."

"And..." Cole glanced at the dining table piled with wedding debris—cards, half-open gifts, leftover decorations, ribbons, taped boxes. "We should probably organize this before it becomes permanent décor."

Ava laughed. "Brittany would haunt us."

"Accurate," Ava laughed. "That sounds exactly like her."

He smiled. "Yeah."

A beat.

Then he straightened. "Want to divide and conquer?"

Ava nodded. "Sure. I'll get started on the gifts."

"And I'll call the airline," Cole said. "And start laundry."

She blinked. "You're going to do laundry?"

"Yeah."

"You know how?"

Cole raised an eyebrow. "Ava. I live alone."

"Okay, but... do you wash delicates separately?"

"Yes."

"Do you clean the lint trap?"

"Yes."

"Do you—"

"You're stalling."

She stuck out her tongue. "Maybe."

Ava plopped onto the couch with her laptop and began sorting cards into neat stacks. Cole disappeared down the hallway with both of their laundry baskets, phone already pressed to his ear.

Ten minutes later, he came back.

Cole rebooked his flight. Ava sorted the wedding gifts, grouping cards with boxes, setting aside anything that still needed tags. He folded the gift-wrap debris into a neat stack. Ava moved the laundry to the dryer without being asked. She made them toast. Cole brewed another round of coffee.

By noon, the house was peaceful.
Domestic.

Safe in a way Ava didn't know how to name.

She leaned against the counter, watching Cole untangle a stack of ribbon.

He looked up at her, catching her staring.
Neither looked away this time.

"Hey," he said softly.

"Hey," she whispered back.

Her heartbeat was too fast.
Too loud.

She cleared her throat. "So… what's next on the list?"

He checked the time. "Lunch?"

"Lunch sounds good."

"And then maybe…" His voice dipped a little, losing its steadiness. "We can figure out what the rest of the week looks like."

A little thrill zipped through her.

Hope.
Fear.
Excitement.

All the dangerous things.

"Yeah," she said. "We should."

Their eyes held.
A beat too long.
A breath too deep.

A moment too honest.

Then Ava smiled—small, shy, and real. Cole smiled back—slow, warm, wrecked.

And both of them knew. Their relationship had changed. Forever.

Lunch was simple—grilled sandwiches, chips, and the kind of easy conversation two people only slip into when something between them has already quietly shifted.

Ava tried not to notice how Cole glanced at her whenever she said something he found funny, like he wanted to say more but didn't. Cole tried not to notice how she bit her lip when she was thinking. Both failed spectacularly.

After cleaning up, Ava sorted the last of the cards while Cole carried wedding gifts to the spare bedroom Brittany had designated as "newlywed storage."

Ava called after him, "Careful with the blender! It's probably expensive!"

Cole's voice floated back, amused. "You're assuming I'm prone to breaking things."

"Are you denying it?"

"No comment."

She snorted and set down a stack of envelopes.

When he came back into the living room, he wiped his hands on his jeans and nodded toward her laptop.

"Everything sorted?" he asked.

She nodded. "Yeah."

"Good."

He leaned on the back of the couch, and for a moment... they just looked at each other.

The kind of look that lasts one second too long. Then another.

Ava cleared her throat and reached for a ribbon. "Okay. What's next?"

"Laundry," he said. "Dryer just buzzed."

"Excellent. I'll supervise."

"You mean critique."

"Same thing."

Cole rolled his eyes but fought a smile as he headed down the hall.

Ava followed, ignoring the slight, inconvenient, traitorous twist in her chest at the sight of him carrying their mixed laundry basket—her clothes mingling with his.

Domesticity shouldn't feel intimate.
And yet.

She swallowed hard and busied herself with folding.

Which went... terribly.
She folded her T-shirts. Fine.
She folded a pair of leggings. Still fine.

Then she reached for one of Cole's T-shirts—soft, warm, smelling like cedar and sleep—and her brain short-circuited.

Cole glanced over. "You okay?"

"Yep!" she chirped, voice cracking. "Totally fine."

[Ava]: Abort mission. He smells unfair. This is illegal.

Cole gave her a look—curious, gentle, amused—then returned to folding.

They worked side by side, brushing hands occasionally, both pretending it wasn't slowly killing them. Not an accident. Not really. Not after the weekend.

By late afternoon, everything was finished.

Laundry put away. Wedding items sorted. Flight rescheduled.

Ava collapsed into the corner of the couch with a sigh. "Well. We survived Monday."

Cole sat on the opposite end—far enough to be polite, close enough that they could easily drift together if either of them stopped being responsible.

"You hungry yet?" he asked.

"A little."

"Leftover wedding mac and cheese?"

Ava gasped. "Yes. A thousand times, yes."

He chuckled. "That enthusiastic about carbs?"

"Always."

Cole stood, grabbing the container and two bowls. "I like that about you."

Ava's heart stuttered hard enough that she felt it in her fingertips.

[Ava]: He didn't mean it like that. Probably. Maybe.

She tucked her legs under herself. "I like... that you can cook without setting the house on fire."

He shot her a grin over his shoulder. "High praise."

Dinner was cozy.
Simple.

Dangerous, in a quiet way, neither addressed.

As the sun set, the house filled with warm golden light. Ava rested her chin on her hand, watching Cole eat, watching him laugh, watching him be comfortable with her in a way that made the knot in her stomach tighter.

Afterward, they washed dishes together—Ava rinsing, Cole drying—bumping hips once by accident.

Both inhaled sharply.
Both pretended they didn't.

When the kitchen was clean, Cole said, "Want to watch something?"

Ava nodded. "Something comforting."

They picked a dumb, overly dramatic cooking competition.

They sat in their usual spots.

And then... slowly... gradually... drifted closer.

Ava shifted, and her blanket slipped, brushing her arm. Cole picked it up gently. He didn't touch her skin. But she felt it anyway.

By the time the third episode started, their knees were touching.

Neither moved. After last night, she couldn't pretend it was nothing.

Ava's pulse thundered. Cole's breath was shallow. They didn't speak about it.

Couldn't.

Finally, after the credits rolled, Ava whispered, "It's getting late."

Cole nodded. "Yeah."

Slowly—painfully—they stood.

He walked her upstairs, stopping just short of her door.

"Goodnight, Ava," he said softly, voice lower than usual.

"Goodnight, Cole."

They lingered—a tiny shift forward, like he almost reached for her again—before stepping back.

Then Ava slipped into her room.
And Cole retreated to his.

Both leaned against their closed doors.
Both closed their eyes.

Both whispered the same thing to empty rooms.

"Oh no."

Because Monday had been... warm.
Playful. Easy.

And overwhelmingly, dangerously not enough. Something in them shifted last night. Today just made it impossible to pretend otherwise.

CHAPTER TEN

Ava woke to the smell of coffee.
Good coffee.

Warm, rich, and way too competent for 7:30 a.m.

She dragged herself into the kitchen, looking like she'd barely survived a mild natural disaster.

Cole, meanwhile, looked like he'd stepped out of a "remote-work-from-home" ad campaign. Barefoot. Hair slightly messy. Calm and annoyingly put-together.

He glanced over his shoulder. Something in his expression paused, softened. "Morning, Aves." Her heart did a small, traitorous flip.

This was already different. And they both knew it.

Ava squinted at the stove. "Are those... pancakes?"

He flipped one with a bit of wrist motion that shouldn't have been attractive but absolutely was. "Found a box in the pantry. Figured we deserved a decent breakfast."

[Ava]: Okay, that's rude. He can't be hot and domestic. Pick one, Cole.

Ava slid onto a barstool and let the warmth of the coffee mug seep into her hands.

When he set a plate in front of her, she stared at it like he'd given her a diamond ring.

"Cole," she whispered dramatically, "I could marry you for this."

He froze—spatula suspended mid-air—as though the feeling of her in his arms flickered through him again.

Ava choked. "I—I mean pancakes. Marry pancakes. Not you. Shut up. I'm eating."

Cole laughed softly, probably saving that moment for future teasing ammunition, and they dug in.

After breakfast, they ran small errands— groceries, a quick pickup of a package Brittany forgot would arrive this week, and a drop-off of leftover wedding decorations.

The grocery store was chaotic.

They split up.
Met at the same aisle.

Split up again.
Met again.

Cole pushed the cart. Ava grabbed a lemon. He accidentally caught her wrist when he reached for the same display.

Both froze. His fingers around her wrist weren't a shock. They were a reminder.

[Ava]: System failure. Reboot immediately.

She cleared her throat. "I just—needed one."

He nodded too fast. "Right. Lemon. Singular. Important."

Ava walked away.

Cole watched her go, rubbed the back of his neck, and muttered to himself, "Get it together."

Back home, they cooked dinner.
Or tried to.

Ava got flour on her cheek.
Cole turned and froze mid-step.

"Ava. Hold still."

She blinked. "What? Why? Is there a bug? Tell me there is not a bug."

He stepped closer and brushed the flour away with his thumb.

Her breath hitched.
So did his.

Then they both stepped back fast, like the counter had shocked them.

"Okay," Ava squeaked, "we're... pretending that didn't happen."

Cole's voice dropped. "Doesn't mean it didn't..."

They resumed cooking.

Very, very carefully.

After dinner, Ava stood by the sliding glass door, watching the pool shimmer under the late-afternoon sun.

She exhaled. "Tomorrow we go back to being functional adults."

Cole stood beside her. "Yeah. Work starts early."

Ava wrinkled her nose. "We should do something fun today. Before we lose our freedom."

Cole followed her gaze to the pool. "You want to swim?"

Her heart fluttered.

Yes.
No.
Yes.

But also no.
Because that meant swimsuits.

And skin.
And proximity.
And she was already at maximum fluster tolerance.

"Sure," she said, too casually. "Why not?"

[Ava]: Idiot.

Ava changed in the guest bathroom.
She stared at her reflection.

[Ava]: It's just a swimsuit. He's seen swimsuits before. He's probably not even thinking about—oh god, this was a terrible idea.

She wrapped a towel around herself and headed outside.

Cole was already in the pool.
And he was—Unfair.

The water slicked down his hair
His shoulders were broad.

Water rolling off his chest in completely illegal ways.

[Ava]: Days of trying not to picture him like this. Useless.

He swam towards the shallow end, pushing up to stand.

"Aves?" he said, blinking at her. "You coming in?"

She swallowed. "Yes. Eventually. In a minute. Maybe."

Cole smiled. "You okay?"

"Nope."

He laughed and splashed water lightly in her direction, the tiniest flick of his fingers.

"Hey!"

"Get in."

She narrowed her eyes. "Make me."

He arched a brow. "Don't tempt me."

Ava's heart fell down an elevator shaft. She stepped to the edge and dipped her toes.

Cold.
Too cold.

She squeaked.

Cole grinned. "Want help?"

"No—Cole!"

He pulled her in.

She surfaced sputtering and laughing, shoving water in his direction. "You menace!"

Cole ducked, splashing her back.
A whole splash war ensued.

Ava shrieked. Cole laughed.
Ava gasped for air. Cole dodged.

It was ridiculous.
It was perfect.

Eventually, they floated near the edge, catching their breath.

The sky glowed orange and pink. The water warmed from the day's heat. Their laughter softened into quiet.

Ava glanced at him.
He was already looking at her.

Her chest tightened with something impossible to name without ruining everything.

"You're—" She stopped. Days of unsaid things were bottlenecked in her throat. "Never mind."

Cole's voice was softer. "What?"

"I don't know," she whispered. "Too much."

His expression shifted. Slow. Warm. Something hungry flickering just beneath the surface.

He moved closer.
Not touching.

But close enough that Ava could feel body heat through the water.

"Maybe we should head in?" she said, breath shaky.

Cole blinked, as if snapping out of something dangerous. "Yeah. Probably."

They both climbed out, dripping and breathless.

Ava wrapped her towel around herself, trying to calm her racing pulse. Cole grabbed his, rubbing it through his hair. Neither looked at the other for a full thirty seconds.

Then Ava laughed softly. "Well. That was fun."

Cole inhaled. "Yeah. It was."

And the way he said it—Not casual. Not light. But almost reverent.

Ava went very still.

[Ava]: Oh. Oh, this is dangerous.

They dried off, changed, and reconvened in the living room for a movie, silently agreeing not to talk about whatever had happened in the pool.

But every time their elbows brushed under the shared blanket...

Every time Cole shifted an inch closer...

Every time Ava leaned her head back, and he followed her motion it was clear they weren't fooling anyone. Especially themselves. Days of pretending not to want this made one inch of contact feel like a fault line shifting.

When the credits rolled, Ava murmured, "We should sleep. Work tomorrow."

Cole nodded. "Yeah."

They stood in the dim hallway.
He hesitated.
She hesitated.

"Goodnight, Aves," he said, voice low and warm—the kind he only used when he stopped guarding himself.

The look he gave her wasn't new. It was the same one she'd been avoiding for two days. "Goodnight, Cole."

They lingered.
Too long.
Then, they turned away.

And neither slept for hours.

CHAPTER ELEVEN

The sun filtered softly through the thin kitchen curtains when Ava padded down the stairs, hair in a messy bun and sweatshirt hanging off one shoulder.

Cole was already at the dining table, laptop open, deep in a video call.

He looked up when he heard her, smiled so faintly she would've missed it if she weren't watching him like a problem she needed and feared in equal measure.

He mouthed, *Morning*.
She mouthed back, *Coffee?*

He pointed to the mug he'd set on the counter.

Ava's chest warmed.

[Ava]: Dammit. Why is he like this? Stop being thoughtful. There really should've been a clause in our remote work agreement about coworkers not being this attractive or this nice before coffee.

She worked from the couch—mostly because she didn't trust herself to sit across from him all day without drooling on her keyboard.

[Ava]: He wasn't a distraction. He was an HR violation waiting to happen.

Cole stayed at the table.

Separate spaces.
Polite distance.

And yet they kept glancing at each other. At the same time. Until one of them looked away too fast, pretending they hadn't.

By late morning, the tension had condensed into something almost... breathable. Almost.

Ava was in a Teams meeting when Cole laughed at something one of his coworkers said—a low, warm, unguarded sound she'd never heard from him before.

Her entire spine straightened.
She forgot she was on camera.

Someone in her meeting asked her a question.

She blinked. "Sorry—what?"

Cole looked over, eyes amused.
She glared at him.

He raised his eyebrows like, *What did I do?*

Ava muttered under her breath, "Illegal."

Cole mouthed, *What?* She deliberately didn't answer.

At lunch, they sat side by side at the counter, picking off the same plate of pasta because neither of them had the energy to pretend they weren't gravitating toward each other.

Ava dropped her fork; it clattered onto the floor.

She knelt to grab it.
Cole knelt at the same time.

They froze, half an inch apart. Like everything they'd been dodging, finally caught up to them.

His breath fanned across her cheek. Her gaze flicked to his mouth—involuntarily.

Cole inhaled, sharply, like she'd touched him. He reached past her slowly, picked up the fork, and set it on the counter without a word.

Neither moved for three long beats.

[Ava]: Back away, Ava. Move. Don't stare at him like that.

But she didn't move first. He did—barely—a subtle shift to give her space.

And somehow that made her want him more. They stood silently, tension simmering between them like something sentient.

The afternoon storm rolled in just as they returned to work.

Thunder cracked hard enough to rattle the windows.

The lights flickered.

Ava yelped—not loudly, but enough for Cole to notice.

[Ava]: *Fantastic. Nothing sexier than a grown woman jump-scaring herself over the weather.*

She instinctively reached for him, fingers curling around his forearm. His muscles tensed under her grip.

He covered her hand with his. Warm. Gentle. Solid.

"You okay?" he asked quietly.

Ava swallowed. "Yeah. Just... jumpy."

He nodded but didn't pull his hand away. Not until she did.

When they separated, both looked anywhere but at each other.

By late afternoon, Ava wandered into the kitchen for a snack. Cole followed a minute later, stretching his back, rolling his shoulders.

"How's work?" he asked.

"Miserable. Yours?"

"Worse."

She laughed softly, and something eased between them—as if they'd remembered how to breathe around each other again.

Cole reached for a mug on the shelf above her. He leaned in. Too close.

His shirt brushed her upper arm for a fraction of a second. Ava's breath caught.

He froze—just long enough for both to feel it.

Then he reached the mug, stepped back, and cleared his throat.

"Sorry," he murmured.

She wasn't.
Not even a little.
She hadn't been for days.

Dinner was simple—grilled chicken, rice, and vegetables. But the way they moved around each other in the kitchen made it feel like choreography.

Cole reached around her for a cutting board, hand grazing her waist.

Ava sucked in a breath.
He stilled.

"I'm—sorry," he whispered.

"It's fine," she whispered back.

They didn't talk much during dinner.
Didn't need to.

Something unspoken had settled between them, thick and warm, impossible to ignore.

After they cleaned up, they migrated to the couch with a blanket and a mindless show.

Shoulders brushed.
Then stayed brushed.

Their legs touched.
Their breathing synced.

Ava rested her head back. Cole's arm drifted behind her on the couch, casual and catastrophically intimate.

Minutes passed like slow molasses. Ava shifted slightly, leaning more into him without realizing. Cole looked down at her. Really looked.

Her eyes lifted to his.
The world went quiet.

"Aves..." he whispered, voice rough.

She felt her pulse everywhere.
She didn't look away.

Neither did he.

He leaned in slowly—painfully slowly—giving her every chance to pull away.

She didn't.

Her palm pressed to his chest—steadying, claiming nothing, feeling everything.

Cole exhaled shakily.
That was it.

The last thread of self-control snapped.

He closed the gap, brushing his lips against hers—careful, questioning...waiting for her to answer.

She did.

Ava kissed him back with a slight, desperate sound she couldn't contain.

Cole groaned quietly—deep, surprised—and the kiss changed instantly, tilting into hunger.

He cupped her jaw gently. She slid her hands into his hair. Their mouths moved together like they'd been waiting for this exact moment.

The show kept playing in the background, forgotten. Cole shifted, pulling her onto his lap without thinking.

Ava gasped.

He paused—just enough to check her eyes.

She nodded.

They kissed again, slower, and deeper. Her fingers tugged his hair. His hands traced her waist.

Heat curled between them like something alive. At one point, he pulled back, breathing hard, forehead resting on hers.

"Ava... we should... slow down..." he murmured, voice unsteady, that low drawl of his melting straight through her.

She nodded, chest rising and falling rapidly. "Yeah. Probably."

But she kissed him one more time.

Lazy.
Soft.
Lingering.

He melted into it.

When they finally stopped, Cole pulled her against him, arms wrapped around her as if it were the most natural thing in the world.

They didn't talk.
No awkwardness.
No panic.

Just warmth and quiet breaths.
Ava rested her head on his chest.

Cole rested his cheek against her hair.

Within minutes, they both drifted off—tangled together under the blanket—the glow of the forgotten TV flickering softly across them.

Ava didn't know when the show had stopped playing. She didn't know how long she'd been asleep. But she knew precisely what woke her.

Warmth.
Heavy, steady, perfect warmth.

Cole's arm was wrapped around her waist. His breath was slow against her temple. His heartbeat thudded softly under her cheek.

She blinked, taking in the dim, quiet room. The living room was all shadows and soft blue light from the microwave clock in the kitchen.

Cole shifted slightly, unconsciously, pulling her a fraction closer.

A helpless, involuntary sound slipped from her throat.

[Ava]: Oh. This is... bad. Dangerous. Perfect. Horrifying. Amazing.

She tilted her chin up. "Cole," she whispered.

He didn't move.

"Cole..." she tried again, brushing her fingers along his forearm.

His breath hitched—the smallest reaction, but enough.

His eyes opened slowly, unfocused and sleepy. He blinked down at her, confusion melting into recognition... and then into something far warmer.

"Aves." His voice was rough and low, a smile crept across his face. He cleared his throat. "What time is it?"

"Late," she murmured. "Really late. We should... go to bed."

He nodded slowly, still half-asleep. "Yeah. Okay."

Then, without fully waking, he moved. One smooth, fluid motion—his body acted before his brain.

He sat up, with his arm still around her, he lifted her with him, keeping her tucked against his chest. She gave a startled little gasp, her hands bracing on his shoulders.

Cole tightened his hold instinctively. "Got you," he breathed, voice deep and thick with sleep.

Ava's heart nearly burst. Before she could say anything more, he stood.

With her still in his arms.

He didn't even seem to think about it. Just rose from the couch, carrying her effortlessly.

Her legs curled up against him, one arm around his neck. She could feel the heat of his skin through his T-shirt, the strength in the effortless way he held her.

[Ava]: Cool. Fantastic. Being princess-carried by a coworker. This had to violate at least three HR policies and one structural beam in self-control.

Her voice came out softer than she intended. "Cole... you don't have to carry me."

He looked down at her—eyes heavy-lidded, hair mussed, expression unguarded and unfiltered.

"I want to," he murmured.

Her whole body flushed.

[Ava]: Oh no. I'm not surviving this man.

He started toward the stairs, adjusting his grip so her body stayed snug against his.

Halfway up, she tucked her face into his shoulder, overwhelmed by the closeness, the warmth, and the way he smelled like cedar and laundry detergent.

He groaned—quiet, almost inaudible—but

she felt it vibrate through his chest.

"You okay?" she whispered.

"Perfect," he said softly.

Ava's breath stuttered.

He reached the top of the stairs and turned toward his bedroom automatically.

Her voice was a shaky whisper. "Cole... my room is—"

"No," he said gently. "Stay with me tonight."

The word *stay* landed harder than it should have. Ava had survived far worse sentences than that. This one nearly undid her.

He nudged his bedroom door open with his shoulder and walked inside, never loosening his hold on her.

He set her down only when they reached the bed—even then, lowering her like she was something breakable. As soon as she touched the mattress, he climbed in beside her, wrapping his arms around her again immediately, as if afraid she might vanish if he let go.

Ava curled instinctively into his chest. Cole exhaled. A deep, relieved sound and pressed his forehead to her hair.

His hand found her hip, fingers splaying gently as he pulled her closer. She whispered, "Cole..."

"Mmm?" His voice was sleep-drenched, soft, honest.

"Are you sure?"

His answer came without hesitation.

"I don't want to let you go yet."

Her heart cracked open.

And before she could overthink it, she tucked her legs between his, fitted her body to his, and let her fingers slide into the soft hair at the nape of his neck.

He groaned again—low, sinful, comfort-laced—and tightened his hold until there was not a sliver of space between them.

His breath ghosted against her cheek. "Goodnight, Aves..."

She smiled against his collarbone. "Goodnight, Cole."

And in the quiet darkness of his room, with Cole's arms around her, she thought one final, quiet truth before sleep pulled her under.

[Ava]: I am so, so done for.

They drifted off like that: entangled, warm, safe, wrapped around each other like they had done it a thousand times before.

CHAPTER TWELVE

Ava woke up to the feeling of being held.

Not metaphorically.
Literally.

She was warm. Cocooned. Something heavy and solid pressed against her back, and there was a very real, very present hand splayed over her stomach.

For half a second, she melted into it.
Then her brain caught up.

Hand.
Arm.
Chest pressed to her spine.

Slow, steady breath against her neck.
Her eyes blinked open in the dim light.

She wasn't in her guest room.
She was in Cole's bed.

And Cole Maddox was wrapped around her like he was her personal weighted blanket.

Ava's heart did a complete somersault.

[Ava]: Okay. Okay. Don't panic. It's fine. It's just... your coworker. Who you made out with. And then climbed into bed with. Totally normal. Everything is fine. This is fine.

Cole shifted behind her, exhaling a low, sleepy sound as his fingers flexed lightly against her stomach. He pulled her just a fraction closer, like his body refused to accept the concept of space.

She swallowed.

"Cole," she whispered.

He didn't answer.

"Cole," she tried again, a little louder, reaching for the hand around her waist.

His thumb moved in the vaguest little stroke against her shirt. He inhaled deeply, blinked his eyes open, and looked down at her.

Confusion flickered.
Then recognition.

Then something softer—something that made her chest ache.

"...hi, darlin'," he murmured, the faint drawl in his voice slipping through—thicker in sleep, warm enough to curl around her spine.

[Cole]: *If she doesn't move, maybe the universe won't notice the catastrophic life choice happening in real time.*

Ava turned in his arms so she could see his face better. "Hi," she smiled.

They stared at each other for a second, neither quite fully awake, both very aware of every single point of contact.

Then realization hit.

Cole cleared his throat and eased his grip, pulling his hand back like it had burned him. "Sorry. I didn't mean to... uh..."

"Use me as a body pillow?" she supplied.

The tips of his ears turned pink. "Yeah. That."

She snorted. "You didn't exactly force me. I stayed."

He blinked at her like that truth had just socked him in the chest. Her cheeks warmed. She immediately regretted saying it out loud.

She pushed the blanket back and slid out of bed, her feet hitting the cool floor. "We should get up. We have work today. And the monthly project meeting."

Cole groaned, flopping a hand over his face. "Right. The meeting I was hoping to attend without a preexisting heart condition."

Ava smirked. "Sorry to ruin your plans."

"You have no idea," he muttered into his pillow.

"What?"

"Nothing," he said quickly, rolling onto his back. "I'm getting up. I'm up. Mostly."

She watched him for one more beat than was reasonable, messy hair, sleepy eyes, the faint mark of her lips still pink on his—and then forced her legs to move toward the door.

"Coffee in fifteen," she said, clinging to the comfort of routine. "Don't be late."

"Yes, ma'am," he replied softly.

And those two simple words made her shiver all the way down her spine.

By the time the meeting rolled around, the house looked deceptively professional.

Ava sat at the dining table, laptop open, headset on. Cole set up across from her in the kitchen, perched at the island like he was in his own home office.

Two coworkers, screens between them.
Nothing unusual.
Totally normal.

If anyone had asked, no one needed to know she'd woken up in his arms forty minutes ago.

The Teams chime sounded.
A grid of little faces popped up.

Project managers.
Developers.
Analysts.
Their boss.

Ava tried to focus. She really did.

But Cole was directly in her line of sight.

He'd rolled his sleeves up. His hair was still slightly damp from his shower. He had that focused expression on, jaw tight, brows furrowed, attention on his screen.

He looked stupidly good.

She dragged her gaze back to her own laptop.

"Welcome to the monthly project briefing," their manager droned. "We've got a packed agenda today, so let's jump right in..."

Her phone buzzed.
A DM from Becky.

Becky: Why do you look like you're watching a slow-motion romance movie?
Becky: You're flushed.
Becky: Who's off camera?

Ava kept her expression neutral and typed under the table.

Ava: I look normal.
Becky: Liar.

Becky: I've seen your "secret crush" face before.
Becky: This is that face.
Ava: New subject.

Across the room, Cole's phone lit up, too.

He glanced at it, lips twitching.
Marcus.

Marcus: Yo.
Marcus: Why are you smiling at your monitor like that?
Marcus: You look like a man who found religion.
Marcus: Who is she?
Marcus: Don't lie.

Cole exhaled slowly through his nose and responded with a single word.

Cole: No.

A beat.
Then:

Marcus: LMAO IT is someone
Marcus: You're a terrible liar.
Marcus: Tell me, or I'm asking in the group chat.

Cole flipped his phone face down and resisted the urge to scrub a hand over his face on camera.

He looked up at the exact moment Ava did. They locked eyes.

She arched a brow. *Everything okay over there?* He gave her a faintly panicked look. *No.* She fought a smile and turned back to her screen.

Their manager moved through the updates team by team. Cole's department went first; he handled his piece with the same calm competence he always did, except Ava could see the subtle tells—the way his throat worked when he swallowed, the way his gaze flicked to her between sentences, like he needed the grounding.

She was no better.

Her stomach fluttered every time he spoke.

By the time their boss said, "Ava, can you give us the status on the client rollouts?" she felt like she'd been holding her breath for half an hour.

She unmuted. "Yep! Sure."

Across from her, Cole shifted in his seat, stretching a little.

His shirt pulled tight across his shoulders. The hem lifted just enough to reveal a strip of tan skin.

Ava's brain blue-screened for a half-second.

[Ava]: Focus.

"So," she began, fingers tightening around her coffee mug, "the onboarding workflow project for Harrington Corp. is about... eighty percent complete. We're waiting on the API patch from engineering before pushing to their testing environment."

She took a breath, reached to set her mug down beside her laptop—and misjudged entirely.

The bottom of the mug landed on the very edge of the table.

It tipped.
Wobbled.
Started to slide.

Ava's heart stopped.

She lunged, barely catching it before it toppled and baptized her laptop in caffeine.

The mug thunked back onto the table with a loud, echoing clatter.

Her mic was on.

There was a beat of startled silence on the call. Then—behind her—just barely off-mic...

Cole snorted.

Of course he did.

The sound cut sharp before he could stop it. His attempt at restraint collapsed into loud, unapologetic laughter in the background.

Human disaster unfolding? Front row seat for Cole Maddox.

His own audio was muted, but it wasn't enough to rein in the laugh that broke free as she panic saved, the sound booming through the meeting before Ava managed to mute herself.

Someone on her team asked, "What was *that*?"

Another voice added, "Because it definitely wasn't feedback."

A third chimed in, "Ava—everything okay on your end?"

She wanted to die.

"Everything is great," she said brightly. "Perfect. Couldn't be better."

On-screen, Cole had completely lost it—shoulders shaking, head ducked, laughter still tearing through him as she shot him a glare just before muting.

He mouthed, *sorry.*

He absolutely wasn't.

She dragged her attention back to the call with the stubbornness of a woman hanging onto her last shred of dignity.

"There are... three main blockers," she forced out. "Documentation gaps for two clients, scheduling conflicts for next Tuesday, and the engineering patch I mentioned."

Her phone buzzed under her hand.
Becky.

Becky: What was that?
Becky: And who just laughed in your house?
Becky: Ava.
Becky: Are you with someone right now?

Ava stared at the camera and gave what was probably the most robotic smile of her life.

"No further updates from me," she squeaked.

"Thanks, Ava," her manager said, already moving on. She slammed her mic back on mute and slumped in her chair.

Across from her, Cole was still looking down at his notes, the corners of his mouth stubbornly tilted up. His eyes lifted just enough to meet hers.

He looked delighted. Fond.
A little wrecked.

Her glare softened despite herself.
She mouthed, *I hate you.*

He mouthed back, *No, you don't.*
Her stomach flipped.

She did not, in fact, hate him.
At all.

Near the end of the meeting, Marcus's voice cut in. "Yeah, I think Cole can speak to that," Marcus said. "He's been... oddly energized today."

Cole's head snapped up. "Marcus."

Their manager chuckled. "Go ahead, Cole."

Cole shot a death glare at his camera—or what passed for one, given the faint flush creeping up his neck—and then launched into more detail about the Harrington Corp. project.

"Right. So, our team's focusing on the new integration timeline. We've identified the major dependencies, and the development branch should be stable by mid-next week..."

Ava barely heard the words.

She watched the way he spoke instead—focused. Confident. One hand gesturing as he explained, the other resting near his keyboard.

He looked like he belonged there.

He always had.

A tiny swell of pride bloomed in her chest, startling and warm.

[Ava]: You are in so much trouble.

Her phone buzzed again.

Becky: Oh my GOD, it's him.
Becky: It's Cole.
Becky: You're into him.
Becky: Tell me it's not Cole Maddox.
Becky: Ava, no.
Becky: Ava, yes!

Ava flipped her phone over and firmly ignored it.

She couldn't do Becky and Cole at the same time. That level of chaos would kill her.

Finally, mercifully, the meeting ended.

The Teams chime sounded, faces disappeared from the grid, and the call dropped away.

The silence that followed was thick and humming and full.

Ava closed her laptop.
Cole did the same.

For a moment, neither said anything.
Then Cole stood.

[Cole]: Okay. Deep breath. ... walk over there casually. Like a normal human. Not like a man who woke up with her in his arms and hasn't been the same since.

He made it halfway across the room before his stomach flipped.

[Cole]: Ava is right there. Why does she look like that? Why does she smile like she knows every thought I'm having and is trying not to laugh at me?

She glanced up.
Their eyes met.

And Cole's brain stopped.

[Cole]: There it is. That look. The one that hits like a punch and a lifeline at the same time. The one I keep pretending I don't crave.

He stepped behind her chair, heart thudding too hard for a man who hadn't done anything except stand near a woman.

[Cole]: Say something. Anything.
Not "you're beautiful in morning light."
Not "come back to bed."
Not "I haven't stopped thinking about your mouth since last night."
Professional. Be professional, you idiot.

He reached out—just barely—letting his fingers graze her shoulder. A single, soft touch.

She shivered.
Cole swallowed hard.

[Cole]: Oh. Oh, that wasn't small. She felt that.

She looked up again, breath catching, eyes soft and open.

And Cole was gone. Completely, helplessly, dangerously gone.

There is no universe where I can sit across from this woman and pretend she's just my coworker again. Not after last night. Not after waking up with her tucked against me like she belonged there. I'm so screwed. So completely, willingly screwed.

He took another slow breath.

"Being in the same room as you," he said softly, "and pretending nothing happened was... impossible."

[Cole]: Understatement of the century, Cole.

Her throat went dry.

"Yeah," she whispered.

He hesitated, then let his fingers trail once—just once—along the top of her shoulder.

A tiny touch.
Barely there.

Her whole body shivered.
He noticed.

His gaze dropped briefly to where his hand had been, then back up to her eyes, darkened with something she recognized now: the same want she'd been trying so hard to bury.

"Aves…"

Her name in his voice did things to her she wasn't ready to unpack.

"Yes?" she breathed.

"We should talk about it," he said, low. "Last night. This. All of it."

Every nerve in her body lit up with equal parts excitement and terror.

"Later?" she asked.

He searched her face. "Later," he agreed.

Her lips curved in a small, helpless smile. "Okay."

He nodded once, straightened a little, and stepped back—not far, but enough to give them both room to breathe.

"I'm gonna grab more coffee," he said, voice a little rougher. "Want another cup?"

"Yeah," she replied. "Please."

He smiled at her—soft, real—before turning to the counter.

Ava watched him move around the kitchen, the familiarity of his presence settling into her like a weight and a comfort all at once.

Her heart was beating too fast.
Her hands were still a little shaky.
Her mind was a mess.

But one thing cut through all the static:
There was no pretending anymore.

Not about what had happened.
Not about what was happening.
Not about how she felt when he looked at her like that.

Later.
Later, they'd talk.
Later, lines would blur even more.

For now, she cradled the coffee he handed her, let her fingers brush his on purpose...and decided she didn't mind being in trouble with

Cole Maddox at all.

Not even a little.

Cole lingered behind her, still close enough that she could feel his presence along her spine.

"Lunch?" he asked quietly.

She glanced up, surprised. "Now?"

He gave a slight shrug. "We're both off-camera. And we haven't eaten."

And I want time with you, his eyes added.

"Yeah," she said softly. "Okay."

They fell into a quiet rhythm in the kitchen, both trying to act normal while absolutely nothing was normal.

Ava grabbed turkey, bread, and fruit. Cole found chips and a cutting board. Their movements kept accidentally syncing—both reaching for the drawer, both stepping in the same direction.

"Sorry—" Ava blurted.

"No, that's on me—" Cole said at the same time.

They froze, half-laughing, half-awkward. His hand brushed her hip as he sidestepped.

Her breath hitched.
He heard it.
Pretended he didn't.

They made two sandwiches, then sat across from each other at the island.

Ava tried to focus on her food, but Cole kept... looking at her.

Not staring.
Just... soft. Aware.

Like he was memorizing everything she did.

She finally set her sandwich down. "What? What."

"What?"

"You're staring."

"I'm not staring."

"You're staring."

His mouth curved. "Okay. Maybe I'm slightly staring."

"Why?"

He didn't answer immediately. Instead, he looked down at his plate, then back up at her.

"You look happy," he said.

Ava blinked. That should not have made her chest squeeze like that.

"Oh." She picked up a strawberry and stared at it way too hard. "Well. I... am. Unfortunately."

Cole's knee nudged hers under the counter.

"Good," he murmured.

They returned to work like two people pretending they weren't in the middle of the strangest, best emotional minefield of their lives.

Cole took his laptop to the living room. Ava stayed at the table.

Both in separate spaces.

They were stealing glances every time they passed by for coffee refills. Every. Single. Time.

Ava called into a short client meeting; Cole's typing stopped the second he heard her voice. He leaned back on the couch, listening—not obviously, but enough that his expression softened every time she explained something.

Cole had his own meeting later, pacing the kitchen as he discussed timelines and deliverables.

Ava heard him through her earbuds and had to actively stop herself from smiling like a maniac whenever he made a joke that landed perfectly.

Every time he walked past her, he brushed her chair. Lightly. Maybe accidentally.

Maybe not.

By the time five-thirty rolled around, Ava's brain felt like static. She closed her laptop and stretched, groaning quietly.

Cole emerged from the hallway a moment later. "We should eat."

"Agreed." She glanced toward the fridge. "We can cook or—"

"Or," he cut in, "I could order something."

She raised a brow. "Like takeout?"

"Like takeout," he echoed. "From the place we passed the other day."

She twisted her lips. "You mean the one with the neon sign that looked like it hadn't been replaced since 1992?"

He grinned. "Yeah. That one."

Ava rolled her eyes, but her chest fluttered. "Fine. You choose."

"Dangerous thing to say," he teased.

Dinner arrived twenty minutes later—stir-fry, fries, dumplings, and something that may or may not have been breaded shrimp.

They sat at the dining table again, closer this time. Their chairs ended up angled toward each other without conscious effort.

Ava shoved a fry into her mouth. "If this gives me food poisoning, I'll haunt you."

Cole smirked. "Promise?"

"Cole."

"I'm just saying. Being haunted by you wouldn't be the worst thing."

She stared at him mid-chew.

He blinked. "I didn't... I don't know why I said that."

Ava swallowed and reached for a dumpling. "You're lucky it was kind of cute."

His eyes softened. "Kind of?"

"Don't push it."

They finished eating.
Cleared the table.
Washed dishes side by side.

And when the kitchen was clean and the house was quiet, Ava wiped her hands on a towel and found Cole watching her.

Not with amusement.
Not with teasing affection.

With something real.
Something unguarded.

"Okay," she said, leaning on the counter. "We said we'd talk."

Cole nodded, setting the dish towel aside. "Yeah. We did."

A moment stretched between them, heavy but not suffocating.

Ava crossed her arms, grounding herself. "So... last night. And this morning. And... all of today."

"A lot," Cole finished.

"Yeah. A lot."

He stepped a little closer, hands braced loosely on the countertop. Not trapping her— just... nearby.

"I'm not good at this," he admitted. "Feelings, talking, being honest. I usually keep everything locked down until it stops existing."

"But this isn't stopping," she said before she could stop herself.

His jaw flexed. "No. It's not."

Silence again.
Warm, charged silence.

Ava took a breath. "Cole... I don't want to pretend nothing's happening."

His shoulders eased just slightly, like he'd been holding something tight all day.

"Me neither."

She offered a small, nervous smile. "That's good. Because I'm terrible at pretending."

He huffed a warm laugh. "Yeah, I noticed."

Ava nudged his arm lightly. "Shut up."

He caught her hand.
Just caught it.

His fingers curled around hers, fitting too easily. Ava's breath stuttered.

"I don't know where this goes," he said quietly. "But I know I don't want it to stop."

Her heartbeat kicked up.

"Me either," she whispered.

Cole's thumb brushed her knuckles. "We'll figure it out. Slowly. Carefully. But... together."

Ava looked down at their hands, then up at him.

"Together," she echoed.

He exhaled—a slow, relieved breath—and stepped half a foot closer.

Not kissing distance.
Not yet.

But near enough that Ava felt her entire body warm. Near enough that he whispered, "Good." Near enough that she whispered back, "Good."

Their hands stayed intertwined until the quiet turned into something soft and new and certain.

And for the first time all day, Ava didn't feel nervous. She felt steady.

She felt sure.
They would talk more later.
They would unravel the rest slowly.

But right now, hands linked, eyes locked, hearts finally aligned—

It was enough.
It was more than enough.

After dinner and their talk, the house felt too warm, too close, too full of things unspoken.

Ava slid the back door open and breathed in the night air. "Want to sit outside for a bit?"

Cole didn't even try to hide the softness in his expression. "Yeah. I'd like that."

They walked to the edge of the pool, settling side by side on the warm concrete. Their feet slipped into the water at the same time—ripples brushing together.

For a while, they just sat there.
Their shoulders bumped once.

Neither of them moved away.

Cole's voice broke the quiet, low and warm. "You doing, okay?"

Ava let out a breathy laugh. "Not even a little."

He smiled softly. "Yeah. Same."

She shifted toward him—just slightly—bringing her knee closer to his beneath the water. He mirrored her without thinking, their bodies angling toward each other like magnets with no sense of restraint left.

"Aves…" he murmured.

She looked up at him just as his hand cupped her cheek. He kissed her—slow at first, soft and careful because he always tried to be gentle with her.

But Ava wasn't in a gentle mood.

A tiny, involuntary sound escaped her throat, and she kissed him harder, leaning in, fingers grabbing his shirt—misjudging her balance entirely.

Her momentum pushed into his shoulder.

He tipped sideways.

Straight into the pool.

"Cole—!" she gasped—and then a wet hand shot up, catching her wrist.

"Oh no," he said, breathless and laughing, water dripping from his lashes, "you're coming with me."

He tugged.

She yelped as she slid off the edge and into the pool beside him with a splash that echoed across the yard.

They surfaced tangled, breathless, laughing directly into each other's mouths.

Ava shoved her soaked hair back, half mortified, half exhilarated. "I didn't mean—"

He kissed her mid-sentence.

Her gasp turned into a muffled sound against his lips as his hands found her waist under the water, pulling her closer—closer than he'd ever allowed himself to imagine.

She curled her fingers into the collar of his soaked shirt, tugging him in, kissing him back with a need that felt startling and right and overdue.

He groaned softly against her mouth. The sound sent heat curling low in her stomach.

They drifted toward the pool's edge, water swirling around them, their bodies brushing under the surface with every breath.

"Ava..." he murmured against her lips, voice low and unraveling, "come inside with me."

She didn't hesitate.
Not even a heartbeat.

She nodded fast.
Breathless
Overwhelmed.

He kissed her again—quick, hungry—then guided them toward the steps, his hand warm and sure at her waist, never letting more than an inch of space exist between them.

They climbed out dripping, clothes clinging, catching each other's mouths in short, heated kisses as they moved toward the sliding door—

—and then into the house, still tangled, laughing, unable to stop.

Ava's back hit the edge of the kitchen counter with a soft thud.

Cole kissed her harder—nothing frantic, just deep, hungry, like he'd been holding back for years. His hands slid to her waist, fingers flexing like he kept stopping himself from lifting her.

Her breath hitched.
He felt it.
His grip tightened.

He broke the kiss only long enough to rest his forehead against hers.

"I can't—get you—close enough."

Before she could answer—before she could even breathe—he pulled her from the counter and kissed her again, guiding her backward toward the stairs like his body refused to allow space between them.

They reached the bottom step, and he turned her, lifting her easily onto the first one.

Her height leveled with his.

Her legs slid between his.

Their mouths met again—slow, deep, melting.

She gasped into his kiss.
His hands tightened on her hips.

He kissed her harder, like he was trying to memorize every sound she made.

And that's when she saw it.
Movement.

Not behind Cole—but over his shoulder, in the entryway.

Ava's breath stuttered painfully.
The front door was open.

Brittany stood frozen just inside the threshold, purse still on her shoulder, suitcase in hand.

Zach stood right behind her, equally stunned, keys dangling from his fingers.

They were both statues.
Horrified, fascinated statues.

Ava whispered, "Cole."

He didn't stop immediately—just slowed, confused. "What? What's—"

She flicked her eyes toward the doorway. Cole turned enough to see—And went utterly still.

Brittany lifted a hand in a stunned, awkward half-wave. "...surprise? We had to change our flight because of the weather. We're home early."

Zach nodded, wide-eyed. "Hi."

Silence fell so dense it was almost comedic.

Ava was perched on the first stair, Cole standing between her knees, his hands on her hips like he'd been seconds away from hauling her upward.

Their friends had just watched the entire migration from patio to counter to stairs in embarrassing, high-definition detail.

Ava's voice came out strangled. "Oh my god."

Zach blinked. "So... we opened the front door expecting darkness, maybe your shoes by the mat... and instead we walked into—"

He gestured vaguely. "All this."

Brittany added, "You two were... very busy."

Ava buried her face in her hands. "No. No— absolutely not—"

Cole dragged a palm down his face. "We didn't hear you come in."

"Oh, we know," Brittany said. "Trust me. You were preoccupied."

Zach crossed his arms. "Honestly? I'm impressed neither of you slipped. The footwork alone was Olympic level."

"Zachary!"

"What? I'm complimenting their coordination."

Ava groaned. "Kill me. Just kill me now."

Cole tried—and failed—to regain dignity. "We were just... uh... heading upstairs."

"Oh, we *got* that part," Zach said.

"No, like—we were talking and then—"

"Buddy," Zach interrupted gently, "nobody is questioning your cardio."

"Zach!" Brittany elbowed him. "Stop. They're mortified."

"I'm mortified!" Ava squeaked.

Cole muttered, "I'm never recovering."

Brittany inhaled, then pointed between them. "Okay. Real question. Are you two together?"

Ava panicked. "We're not—"

Cole said at the same time, steady and sure, "We are."

Ava whipped her head toward him. He gave a small, unapologetic shrug.

Brittany shrieked. "I knew it!"

Zach sighed dramatically. "Cool. Great. Love it for you guys. But not on my stairs."

Ava melted backward onto the step. "I hate everything."

Cole sat beside her, shoulder brushing hers. "Worth it," he murmured.

Her stomach flipped traitorously hard.

Brittany grabbed her suitcase. "Okay! We're gonna go unpack, pretend we didn't witness a Cinemax special, and let you two... breathe."

Zach nodded. "And Maddox? Sanitize whatever that was."

"Zachary!" The front door clicked shut behind them. They headed for their bedroom, still bickering.

Silence dropped.

Ava covered her face. "I am never showing my face again."

Cole exhaled a shaky laugh and leaned slightly closer. "I still want to take you upstairs."

"Cole."

He shrugged, helpless. "What? I didn't say we should. I said I still want to."

Ava groaned. "You're impossible."

Cole nudged her knee gently, voice warm and ruinous. "And you're trouble."

Her heart sank and soared at the same time.

CHAPTER THIRTEEN

Cole woke to an unfamiliar feeling.
Peace.

No alarm. No buzzing anxiety. Just the muted hum of a quiet house and the soft realization that there was someone on the other side of the hall he wanted to see more than coffee.

He lay there for a moment, staring at the ceiling, replaying the way Ava had laughed last night. The way Brittany's dramatic gasp still rang in his ears. The way he'd called her *trouble...* and meant it in the best way.

Yeah. Sleep was officially over.

Cole padded across the hall and stopped outside Ava's door, hesitating for half a second before lifting his hand.

Knock. Knock.
A faint shuffle.

"Come in," Ava's voice called, thick with sleep.

He eased the door open.

She was still curled beneath her blankets, hair wild, eyes just barely open—soft in that fragile, just-woken way that hit him straight in the chest.

[Cole]: God, she's beautiful.

Cole crossed the room quietly and perched on the edge of the bed.

"Morning, sleepyhead."

She blinked at him. "What time is it?"

"Late enough, you don't have to pretend to be productive."

She smiled at that.

Before either of them fully realized what was happening, he leaned down and kissed her.

Soft.
Unthinking.
Natural.

Her lips curved into his almost instantly.
And then he froze.

Pulled back just enough to think.

"—Hey. That's okay, right?"

Ava let out a breathy little laugh and reached up to curl her fingers into the front of his shirt.

"Yes," she said warmly. "That's definitely okay."

Relief washed through him like a warm exhale.

He slid fully onto the bed beside her, staying careful, giving her space—though she promptly ignored it by nestling into his side anyway, her head fitting where it apparently belonged beneath his shoulder.

They lay there wrapped together without urgency, the kind of closeness that didn't need fixing or defining yet.

"What do you wanna do today?" she murmured.

He thought for a second. "Not think about anything stressful."

"Excellent plan," she approved. "I vote breakfast and zero responsibility."

Cole laughed. "Works for me."

Neither of them moved immediately.
This was too good.

Eventually, Ava sighed dramatically. "Okay, fine. Let's go face the world."

They climbed out of bed reluctantly and headed downstairs, fingers brushing constantly—unable to walk more than a foot apart even in the tiny hallway.

Brittany clocked them immediately.
Of course she did.

She was cracking eggs into a bowl when Ava and Cole entered the kitchen—Cole leaning down to brush a gentle kiss to Ava's temple on impulse.

A pause.
The bowl stopped mid-crack.

"Oh, this is *happening*," Brittany said brightly.

Zach looked up from the coffee machine and just shook his head, smiling. "Called it. Years of timing disasters, and the second you two end up in the same place..."

Ava's cheeks warmed instantly. "We're not— that's not—"

Cole smiled and finished calmly, "We're just... seeing where this goes."

Brittany beamed.

"About time," she declared.

Breakfast unfolded easily—teasing, laughter, the faintest air of shared secret between Ava and Cole that neither of them seemed able to stop broadcasting.

He brushed his thumb over her knuckles when he passed her a plate. She stole quick kisses when she thought no one was watching.

Nothing inappropriate.
Just... constant.

Zach noticed, smirking into his coffee.

"So," he said casually, "what I'm seeing is about fifteen seconds between affectionate incidents."

Brittany elbowed him. "Let them be cute."

They did.
Relentlessly.

Later, when Brittany and Zach left to run errands, Ava and Cole gravitated back to the couch.

No show this time.
Just proximity.

Cole's thumb traced slow comforts into the back of her hand.

"This still, okay?" he murmured.

She nodded. "Yeah."

And she meant it.

They didn't talk about long-distance.
Didn't talk about work complications.
Didn't touch the future at all.

They just existed in this perfect pocket of something new and fragile and exciting.

When late afternoon finally pushed them apart—Ava for a shower, Cole to wander restlessly into the kitchen—he stopped.

"Hey," he said quietly as he closed the distance between them.

She turned.
He kissed her—gently, and deliberately.

Not rushing.
Not crossing lines.

This time thinking every step—and still choosing to do it.

"How did we wait this long for something this easy and good?" he murmured, warmth threading his voice in a way that pulled her closer.

Her smile came soft and unguarded. "Yeah," she said quietly. "I don't know how we did."

She walked away with light in her chest that she didn't try to dim.

That night, as she curled beneath her blankets, regretting not sharing a bed, she fell asleep smiling.

—And then the sound came.

CHAPTER FOURTEEN

Not too loud.
Not a shout.

More like a ragged breath forced through a clenched throat.

Ava's eyes snapped open.

Another followed—lower this time, pained, almost strangled.

It came from across the hall.
Cole's room.

Ava sat up immediately, pulse spiking.

For half a second, she hesitated—because going into your coworker-turned-something's room after almost hooking up on the stairs felt like voluntarily walking into a hurricane—but then another sound broke through the quiet.

A choked, barely-there, "No... don't—"

That was enough.

Ava was already on her feet before her mind caught up. She crossed the hall and knocked, whispering urgently.

"Cole?"

Nothing.

"Cole, it's Ava—can I come in?"

Still nothing. Just the harsh rustle of sheets and an uneven, panicked breath.

She didn't wait.
Ava pushed the door open.

Moonlight spilled across the room, painting everything in cold blue.

Cole was tangled in the blankets, chest rising too fast, brow furrowed tight, fists knotted in the sheets like he was holding onto something that wasn't there.

His voice came again, tight and faraway.

"Emery? Emery—wait—"

A punch of fear hit her chest.

Ava stepped closer, voice soft but steady. "Cole... you're dreaming."

He flinched—hard—like he was reliving something he couldn't escape.

Ava reached out and touched his arm.
He jolted upright with a sharp gasp.

Not awake.
Not fully.

His eyes were wide, searching the room like he didn't know where he was.

"Hey," Ava whispered quickly, hands lifted a little to show she wasn't trying to crowd him. "Cole. It's okay. You're safe. You're here."

His breath stuttered—still too fast—but his gaze finally found her, recognition slowly settling in.

"Ava…" His voice was rough, scraped raw from the dream. He dragged a shaking hand through his hair. "Shit. I didn't mean to wake you. I was just—"

"You didn't." She climbed onto the edge of the mattress, careful not to startle him. "Look at me."

He did.

And God, the look in his eyes—shaken, exhausted, guilty for something that wasn't his fault—hit her like a weight.

Ava moved closer without thinking. "Do you want to talk about it?"

"No," he murmured, throat tight. "Not yet."

She nodded once. "Okay."

Silence fell—soft, fragile, settling between them like a blanket neither of them asked for.

Cole exhaled slowly, each breath steadier than the last. His shoulders lowered an inch at a time, like he was coming back into his own skin.

"Do you... want me to stay until you fall asleep?" she asked.

His expression cracked—barely, but enough to show how much the question hit him.

"Aves," he whispered, voice breaking around the edges, "you don't have to."

"I know." She eased closer, sitting hip-to-hip beside him. "But do you want me to?"

He didn't answer with words. He just let out a breath—small, shaky—and nodded.

Ava leaned her shoulder against his, grounding him. "I'm here."

Cole's head tipped toward her instinctively, like gravity had its own agenda.

He wasn't holding her—not really—but his whole body leaned toward her warmth.

Minutes passed.
His breathing slowed.
The tension in his jaw softened.

His hand on the mattress relaxed until his pinky brushed hers—barely there, but unmistakably deliberate.

A quiet beat passed before he murmured, almost too soft to hear:

"Thank you... for coming in."

Ava's chest tightened.

"Always," she whispered back.

They stayed like that—shoulders touching, breaths syncing—until sleep finally pulled him under again.

Ava stayed a little longer, watching the calm return to his face, making sure he was okay.

Only when she was certain did she stand, slipping quietly back across the hall and into her room.

But as she lay in the dark, heartbeat still unsteady, one truth echoed through her chest with a clarity she wasn't ready for.

She was already in too deep.
And she wasn't sure she wanted out.

CHAPTER FIFTEEN

A soft knock pulled Ava from sleep.

Not loud.
Not hurried.
Just... careful.

"Aves?"

Cole's voice—low, worn, unsure.

Ava pushed up onto her elbows. "Yeah?"

The door opened an inch, then wider as Cole stepped inside holding a tray—coffee, scrambled eggs, toast, and fruit. He looked painfully uncertain, like he wasn't sure if crossing her doorway was allowed anymore.

"I, uh... made breakfast."

A slight, almost nervous shrug.

"For last night. And for... waking you."

Ava warmed immediately. "You didn't wake me."

"You still came in," he said softly, setting the tray across her lap. "You didn't have to. But you did."

She swallowed. "Of course I did."

Cole sat slowly on the edge of the bed, elbows braced on his knees like he wasn't sure if he was supposed to stay or leave.

Ava took a sip of the coffee—perfect, exactly how she liked it. "Do you... want to talk about it?"

His jaw flexed once.
Then, after a beat, he nodded.

"It's not just a nightmare," he said quietly. "It's a memory. One that... still gets me sometimes."

Ava's chest pulled tight. "Okay. I'm listening."

Cole exhaled slowly through his nose, eyes fixed on his hands.

"When I was a kid—maybe eight or nine—my sister and I used to explore the woods behind our house. Not real trails, just thick pines and underbrush and these old logging paths that disappeared if you weren't paying attention."

Ava pictured it instantly: two kids, mud on their boots, oversized backpacks, innocence and adventure.

"One afternoon, we wandered deeper than we ever had before. We didn't notice how fast the sun was dropping. We were messing around—climbing deadfall, looking for frogs—stupid stuff kids think is adventure."

His voice thinned slightly.

"And then... we got separated."

Ava's breath caught. "Separated how?"

"There was this old drainage dip," he said, eyes distant. "You couldn't see it from the trail—it looked flat until you were right on top of it. My sister crossed first. I went to follow but... I slipped."

He swallowed hard.

"Just a couple of feet down. But when I scrambled up again... she wasn't there. I couldn't see her. Couldn't hear her. And the woods got... really big. Really fast."

Ava's heart twisted.

"I shouted for her. She shouted for me. But it kept getting darker, and every sound felt wrong. I didn't know which direction was home. I didn't know where she was. All I could think was... I lost her. I messed up. And nobody was going to find either of us."

He scrubbed a hand over his face.

"By the time she found her way back to me—maybe twenty minutes later—I was a wreck. And she—" A tiny breath of a laugh. "She clung to me so hard I couldn't breathe. I think I scared her more than she ever admitted."

Ava blinked hard, fighting sudden heat in her eyes.

"That's... a lot for a kid," she whispered.

"Yeah." He nodded, voice low. "And every once in a while, it comes back in my sleep. Not the whole thing—just that feeling of calling out and not knowing where she is. Or where I am."

Ava reached out and gently covered his hand.

"You were just a kid," she murmured. "No one expects an eight-year-old to know how to get home through the woods."

Cole huffed a tired half-laugh. "Tell that to my sister. She didn't let me out of her sight for months after that."

Ava softened. "That makes sense. Fear like that gets into your bones."

He didn't say anything for a moment, just stared at their hands, her fingers resting lightly over his.

"Sometimes," he said quietly, "it still feels like I'm back there. Yelling into the trees. Knowing she can't hear me."

Ava's heart tightened. "That sounds terrifying."

"It was," he admitted. "And I hate that it still shows up like this. Especially when there are people around."

"You don't have to apologize," she said gently. "Nightmares aren't something you control."

He let out a slow breath, something inside him easing—barely, but enough.

"Thank you," he murmured. "For waking me up. For staying."

Ava's voice gentled. "Anytime."

They stayed like that for a quiet moment, close without crowding, steady without pushing, the morning light soft around them, the air full of everything they hadn't said yet.

And everything they were about to.

A beat of silence stretched—gentle, warm—until Ava finally nudged the tray.

"Okay," she said, trying to lighten the air, "I need to address something very important."

Cole blinked. "Yeah?"

She held up a forkful of eggs. "These are... suspiciously good."

He huffed a laugh. "Suspiciously?"

"No normal human makes this at..." she checked the clock on her phone, "...7:04 a.m. Did you bribe a chef?"

Cole rolled his eyes. "It's eggs, Ava. You whisk. You cook. You don't burn."

"Well," she sniffed dramatically, "some of us have a more... interpretive relationship with stovetops."

"Interpretive?"

"Creative."

"Aves," he said with a soft laugh, "you once told me you burned oatmeal."

"That pot betrayed me."

"Oh, absolutely," he deadpanned. "The pot. Classic villain arc."

She tried to glare but ended up smiling instead.

He nodded toward her coffee. "At least the caffeine is right."

She took a sip. "Okay, yeah, the coffee is perfect too. Jerk."

Cole smiled into his hands. "You're welcome."

Ava stabbed a strawberry. "So, you're just... this good at breakfast? At seven a.m.? After a nightmare?"

He lifted a shoulder. "Chaos coping mechanism."

She snorted. "Mine is buying notebooks I never use. Yours is... being unnervingly functional."

"Functional?" He widened his eyes. "Wow. Harsh."

She nudged his knee with hers. "You know what I mean."

"Mm." He glanced at her plate. "Are you gonna eat the toast or keep interrogating me about eggs?"

"I can do both," she declared proudly.

"Of course you can."

She made a face at him, and he made one back. For a moment, it felt like them—warm, easy, and comfortable.

Too comfortable.

Ava felt the shift before it happened—like the laughter thinned, the air stilled, and the thing they'd both been avoiding crawled right back between them.

Her smile faded first.
Cole's followed.

He looked down at his hands, then at her, something bracing in his eyes.

"Aves..." he said quietly.

"Yeah," she murmured, heart tightening, "I know."

The air changed.
Lightness slipping away.

The real conversation settled over them like a heavy truth they couldn't dodge anymore.

They were both going home tomorrow—back to the real world, back to routines, back to whatever they were before this week cracked everything open. It should have felt grounding. Normal.

But it didn't.

Ava couldn't shake the concern that had been tugging at her this whole time.

Distance.

It pulsed in her chest, steady and cold, the familiar ache of something she'd lived through once already and barely survived.

She set her fork down, fingers tightening around the edge of the tray.

"Cole..." she started, then stopped. Tried again, softer. "I keep thinking about... what happens after today."

He went very still.

A flicker of understanding—resignation, crossed his face. "Yeah. Me too."

Ava exhaled a shaky breath, staring at the blanket pooled around her legs. "I tried a long-distance relationship once. In college."

He didn't interrupt.
Didn't push.
Just waited.

"It was with my high school boyfriend. Someone I thought I knew inside out. Someone I..." She swallowed. "It doesn't matter. What matters is how it ended."

Cole shifted, turning toward her completely. "You don't have to—"

"I do." Her voice cracked, just a little. "He cheated. Twice. And when I found out... I spiraled. Bad. I wasn't sleeping, I wasn't eating, I wasn't functioning. It took me months—months—to feel like a person again."

She rubbed her thumb along the edge of the tray, grounding herself.

"So, when I think about long distance now... even with someone I trust... I feel like I'm back there. Like I'm waiting to fall apart again."

Cole absorbed that in silence—deep, thoughtful, pained silence—before finally speaking.

"Aves," he said quietly, "I would never do that to you."

Her throat tightened. "I know."

"But," he finished, voice low, "it doesn't change what it did to you."

She nodded, eyes burning.

He wasn't defensive.
Wasn't arguing.

Just... seeing her.

"But that's only half of it," she continued, pushing through the tightness in her chest. "You have your own reasons, too. You told me once you avoid anything that looks like a workplace romance because it blew up on you before."

Cole's jaw flexed.
A muscle in his cheek ticked.

He didn't look away.

"Yeah," he admitted, voice rough. "And I told myself I'd never tangle my personal life with my career again. It cost me a job I cared about. My reputation. My confidence. Took a long time to rebuild all that."

He rubbed his palms together, a restless, grounding motion.

"And now... here you are. And I—" He broke off, exhaling sharply. "I don't want to screw up your life. Or mine. Or the job you love."

Something inside Ava twisted.

Because every piece of him sounded like the truth. And every piece of her wanted to lean forward anyway.

She tucked her knees up, whispering, "So, what do we do?"

He met her eyes.
Long, aching, honest.

"We stop, before it goes too far," he said quietly.

Her chest cracked.

She nodded, though it hurt. "Yeah. We stop."

Even though her heart was screaming the opposite. Even though the week was still on her lips and in her bones.

Even though the version of them that lived in the dark, tangled under blankets and moonlight, felt impossibly right.

Cole's voice softened. "Not because I don't want you."

The confession broke something inside her and soothed it at the same time.

"And not because I don't want you," Ava whispered.

They sat there in the quiet, both pretending their hearts weren't breaking a little.

Both pretending this choice didn't feel like ripping out something that had barely begun.

Finally, Cole stood, straightening slowly. "Do you want... help getting downstairs?"

Ava let out a small, humorless laugh. "If I go down there looking like this, Brittany is going to sniff out emotional carnage from a mile away."

He managed a faint smile. "You could pretend you're just sad about the eggs being gone."

"That would be believable."

He held out a hand for the tray, careful not to brush her fingers when he took it.

A distance they both hated but needed.
For now.

"Take a minute," he said softly. "I'll go start more coffee."

She nodded.

He hesitated in the doorway, as if something inside him was begging to turn back.

But he didn't.
He left.

And Ava stayed in the quiet room, breathing through her shaky exhale, knowing the truth neither of them said out loud:

Stopping wouldn't make the feelings disappear.

It would just make them hurt quieter.

CHAPTER SIXTEEN

Ava waited until her breathing felt passably normal before heading downstairs.

The scent of coffee drifted up the stairwell—warm, steady, and comforting. Too comforting. The kind that made everything ache.

She padded into the kitchen.

Cole was at the counter, measuring out creamer with clinical precision, shoulders held in that careful, neutral way he used whenever he was trying to keep himself together.

He looked up briefly when she entered.

Just a flicker.
A polite smile.
Nothing like yesterday.

Her chest pinched.

Before either of them could speak, the patio door slid open.

Brittany breezed in, wearing a messy bun, pajama shorts, and the expression of someone who woke up ready for gossip. Zach followed behind, carrying two travel mugs and a look of mild existential concern. They both froze when they saw Ava and Cole. The tension in the room was no longer a quiet, private thing.

It was a *weather system.*

Brittany blinked once.
Twice.

Her eyes ping-ponged between Ava and Cole like she was watching a tennis match played entirely with micro expressions.

"...Good morning?" Brittany said, voice unnervingly gentle. Too gentle. Suspiciously gentle. "Sleep well?"

Ava forced a smile. "Yep. Great."

"Totally," Cole added, nodding like an animatronic human.

Zach leaned against the doorframe, squinting.

"You two look... rested," he said slowly.

A statement that was both accurate and a blatant lie at the same time.

Brittany elbowed him. "Stop narrating."

"I'm observing," Zach whispered loudly.

Brittany plastered on a bright smile and, in the most unsubtle attempt at casual conversation ever performed by a human being, asked:

"So, how's everybody's... emotional stability this morning?"

Ava choked.

Cole coughed into his coffee.

Zach muttered, "Good lord, Brittany."

"What? I'm checking in!" she hissed.

Ava grabbed her own mug. "I'm fine."

"I'm good," Cole echoed.

They said it too quickly.
Too evenly.
Too identically.

Zach raised an eyebrow. "Wow. That was... synchronized."

Brittany crossed her arms. "Okay. Nope. Something is weird."

Ava froze. "Nothing's weird."

Cole: "Nothing at all."

Zach gestured between them. "You're standing three feet apart like two coworkers at a corporate mixer who don't want HR to get the wrong idea."

Brittany leaned forward, lowering her voice. "The other night, you two were practically *fused* before we walked in."

Ava's cheeks warmed with embarrassment, but the quick sting of sadness flickered across her features before she could hide it. "We don't have to talk about that."

"Oh, I think we do," Brittany said.

"Babe," Zach murmured, "give them some privacy."

"No. They're acting like we hallucinated the whole stairway make-out marathon. I need clarity."

Ava rubbed her forehead. "We just... talked."

Brittany's eyes narrowed. "That is not a 'we made out on a staircase' face. That is a 'someone emotionally imploded' face."

Cole flinched so subtly that only Ava caught it.

She straightened. "Brittany... can we not do this right now?"

Her friend hesitated for just a moment—and Ava saw the shift. Concern overtook curiosity.

"Hey," Brittany said more softly. "Are you okay?"

Ava nodded quickly. "Yeah. We ... have things to figure out. And we're... taking some space."

Zach's eyebrows shot up in sympathy. "Oof. Space."

Cole cleared his throat. "It's for the best."

Brittany's expression softened. "Okay. Then we'll... respect that."

Zach clapped his hands once. "Group decision: nobody talks about feelings until at least after breakfast. Preferably after noon."

Ava exhaled, relieved. "Thank you."

"Ground rules," Zach continued. "No relationship interrogations, no stairway flashbacks, and absolutely no recreations of the scene for educational purposes."

"Zachary!"

"What? They're adults! I'm being supportive!"

Ava let out a small laugh—surprised, grateful.

Brittany rubbed her arm. "We love you. Both of you. And whatever's going on... tell us if you need anything."

Ava nodded, chest tight but steady. "I will."

Cole echoed a quiet, "Same."

The four of them moved around the kitchen after that—awkward, gentle, trying not to step on emotional landmines—and though the air was still a little off-balance.

The pressure eased.

At least enough to breathe.

Enough for Ava to refill her coffee. Enough for Cole to stand on the opposite side of the island without cracking.

Enough for Brittany and Zach to exchange a glance that said we're watching them, but we're not pushing.

The rest of the morning passed in stiff, polite silence.

Brittany and Zach had plans—lunch with friends, dinner with family still in town from the wedding—so they slipped out mid-morning with a cheerful, "Try not to burn the house down."

Ava didn't answer.

Cole barely looked up from wiping an already clean counter. The second the front door shut, silence collapsed over them again.

Ava grabbed her jacket. "I'm going for a walk."

Cole nodded once, jaw tight. "Be safe."

She left without another word.

Cole stood there a long moment, hands braced on the sink, head bowed like the weight of the entire week was balancing between his shoulder blades.

Then he moved.
Fast.

He vacuumed.
Loaded the dishwasher.
Wiped down the kitchen twice.
Organized the mail that wasn't his.

Folded a blanket.
Unfolded it.
Folded it again.

Anything to keep busy. Anything to keep from thinking.

Ava returned an hour later, cheeks flushed, expression unreadable. She slipped upstairs. Cole pretended not to watch her go.

The afternoon didn't get any less painful. They drifted through the house like strangers.

Separate rooms.
Separate workflows.
Separate everything.

When hunger finally forced them from isolation, fate personally grabbed the wheel and steered chaos straight into their faces.

Ava opened her guest-room door at the exact moment Cole opened his.

They froze.
Again.

She lifted a takeout menu. "I'm ordering dinner."

Cole lifted his phone. "I already did."

They both stepped aside in the hallway.
They both stepped in the same direction.
Then the other.

Ava groaned. "I swear to God, we're clinically defective."

Cole's mouth twitched. "Mismatched Roombas."

She choked out a reluctant laugh, covering her face with her hand before it betrayed too much.

Fifteen minutes later, two separate delivery drivers arrived—one knocking on the front door, one ringing the doorbell.

Ava moved toward the kitchen island with her bag. Cole stepped toward the counter with his.

They opened their takeout containers.
Then both paused.

Ava held up his pad Thai.
Cole held up her tacos.

They stared at each other.
A beat.

Then Ava muttered, "Of course."

Cole huffed a soft laugh, pushing the wrong container toward her. "At least the universe is consistent."

She took it without letting their fingers touch.

They ate separately—Ava perched at the island, Cole at the dining table—close enough to hear the scrape of each other's forks, far enough to feel like continents were between them.

By the time darkness settled, the house felt too big and too small all at once.

At 9:17 p.m., the front door clicked open.

"Hello house gremlins!" Brittany announced cheerfully as she burst inside, still glowing from dinner. Zach followed, carrying leftover containers and high spirits.

Ava stiffened on the couch.
Cole straightened instinctively.

Brittany froze mid-stride. Her eyes snapped between the two of them once, twice.

"Oh, absolutely not," she declared. "What is this energy?"

Zach sniffed. "Smells like denial."

"Zachary!"

"What? I'm right."

Ava stood. "Nothing happened."

Cole said at the same time, "Everything's fine."

Brittany planted her hands on her hips. "Both of you sound like two middle-schoolers who got caught passing notes."

She pointed at Ava. "Kitchen. Now."

"Britt—"

"Don't Brittany me. Conference room. Emergency meeting."

Ava shot Cole an apologetic look as she was dragged away.

Zach dropped onto the couch beside Cole. "So... beer?"

Cole sighed. "Yeah. I'll go grab them." He headed to the garage.

Brittany didn't even wait for the doorway.

"What happened?" she hissed.

Ava blinked. "Nothing. We just... talked."

"About?"

Ava hesitated.

Brittany softened immediately. "Oh no. Honey. Tell me."

"It's just…" Ava exhaled shakily. "We're both going home tomorrow. And I'm scared."

"Of what?"

"Distance," Ava whispered. "Long-distance relationships wrecked me once. I barely survived it. I can't… I can't do that again."

Brittany's face crumpled with sympathy.

"Oh, Aves. He is not Nathan."

Brittany's expression softened even more. She stepped closer, placing her hands on Ava's arms.

Ava nodded, eyes stinging. "I just… don't want to screw things up. With anyone."

What she didn't know—what she couldn't know—was that Cole had stopped just around the corner.

He had two beers in his hands. He hadn't meant to listen. He'd only meant to walk in and hand one to Zach.

But the second he heard Brittany softly say, "You're allowed to want something for yourself, Ava," he froze.

Then Ava's voice, quiet and ragged.

"I don't survive losing people. Not again. Not someone I—"

Her voice broke off.
Cole's heart did the same.

Zach's voice floated from the living room: "Bro? You die in there?"

Cole blinked, stepping back before he was caught.

"Yeah," he called, voice thin. "Coming."

He forced himself to walk away even though every part of him stayed rooted against the wall.

Zach accepted a beer with a grin. "So? Feeling better?"

Cole took a long drink. "No," he said honestly. "Not even close."

By the time the house went quiet again, exhaustion was the only thing either of them had left.

Ava brushed her teeth, folded tomorrow's clothes on the chair, and double-checked her boarding pass. All the small, practical rituals she clung to when her chest felt too tight.

Across the hall, she heard Cole doing the same. A zipper closing. Footsteps shifting. A soft, frustrated exhale that hit her right in the ribs.

Two people getting ready to leave the same house...and step back into entirely different lives.

Ava turned off her lamp. For a long moment, she stared at her door.

She could open it.
Just say goodnight.
Just make sure he was okay.

But that tiny crack in her chest—the one she'd been desperately trying to close—kept her still.

She stayed in bed.

A quiet knock tapped on the other side of her door.

Not a question.
Not an invitation.
Just... him.

Ava held her breath, her heart beating too loud in the dark.

She didn't open it.
He didn't knock again.

But she felt him there—the weight of his hesitation, his uncertainty, the same ache she was fighting, before the floorboards creaked softly and he walked away.

Ava lay back, staring at the ceiling, hands curled into the blankets.

She told herself this distance was the wise choice.

So why did it feel like she'd just let something slip through her fingers?

CHAPTER SEVENTEEN

Cole didn't sleep.
Not really.

He drifted in and out, the cheap guest-room ceiling fan clicking with every rotation, each sound reminding him he only had a few hours left in this house. In this city. Near her.

By the time the first faint light crept through the blinds, he gave up.

He finished packing in silence, trying not to think. Trying not to picture her sleeping across the hall, curled under that too-big blanket she'd stolen from Brittany's couch. Trying not to replay every moment of last night, every glance, every space they intentionally kept between them.

At 6:10 a.m., he zipped his suitcase.

At 6:15 a.m., he stood in the hallway.

Ava's door was cracked open an inch as he approached, just enough for the unmistakable rasp of her snoring to reach him.

He stepped closer, suitcase handle in one hand, his heart in the other.

He could knock.
He could wake her.

He could say goodbye properly.

One last moment before everything went back to screens and distance and pretending.

He hovered there for a full minute.
Maybe two.

His hand lifted a fraction toward her door.
Then he froze.

[Cole]: *Don't make this harder for her. Don't make it harder for yourself. You already decided. You both did. Walk away.*

He swallowed hard and forced his hand down. "Bye, Aves," he whispered—so quietly it barely existed.

He left before he could change his mind.

Down the stairs.
Out the door.

Into the waiting rideshare.
Not looking back.

Ava woke to silence.
Thick, heavy, unnatural silence.

For a disoriented second, she didn't remember what day it was. Or why her chest hurt. Or why her eyes felt tight and swollen.

Then it hit.
Sunday.

Going home.
Going back to normal.

She sat up slowly, the ache settling deep in her ribs.

[Ava]: I don't want to leave. I don't want to stay. I don't like this decision we made. I don't know what I want except him, and I can't have that.

She stood on shaky legs and opened her door, expecting—desperately hoping—to hear Cole's door open across the hall, to see him half-asleep and rumpled and painfully handsome in the morning light.

The hall was empty.

His door stood wide open.
His room was spotless.
His suitcase is gone.

Ava's hand flew to her mouth as a sharp, quiet sound escaped her.

He left.
He left without waking her.

Without a goodbye.
Without anything.

She stumbled towards the stairs and sank onto the top step, gripping the railing until her knuckles turned white.

[Ava]: This is what we wanted. This is the right choice.

It didn't stop the cracked, hollow feeling spreading through her chest.

Eventually, she stood.

Washed her face. Packed on autopilot. Wrote a goodbye note for Brittany and Zach.

Ordered her own rideshare.
Locked the house behind her.

Each action felt like moving underwater.

Zombie-like.
Directionless.
Numb.

Both of their days unfolded in parallel, though neither knew it.

Cole sat in the back of his Uber, forehead against the window, watching the city blur past. His phone was dark in his hand, the message he'd typed to her sitting unsent.

Have a safe flight.
It was good seeing you.
I'm sorry.
I miss you already.

He deleted every draft.

At the airport, he moved through security automatically, barely responding when the TSA agent asked him to step forward.

He boarded early.
Sat by the window.
Closed his eyes.

Pretended he didn't feel like something had been carved out of him.

Ava walked through the airport clutching her carry-on like it might hold her together.

Check-in blurred.
Security blurred.

The gate announcement blurred. She sat at her window seat, staring at the tarmac, throat tight.

[Ava]: I should've gotten up earlier. I should've said goodbye. I should've—

But every thought ended the same.

[Ava]: He left. He left because we told him to.

She pressed her forehead to the cool window and let her eyes close.

Cole's plane touched down first.

He took another Uber home, dropped his bags in the entryway, and didn't turn on a single light.

He just walked to his room, collapsed backward onto the bed, and stared at the ceiling.

He could still smell her shampoo on his shirt.

Move on, he told himself.

But his chest ached like he'd been cracked open with a dull blade.

Hours later, Ava stepped into her studio apartment, dropped her suitcase, and sank face-first onto her bed.

Her pillow smelled like detergent, and nothing like him.

She didn't cry.

She just lay there, staring at the wall, feeling the weight of everything they didn't say.

Everything they wanted.
Everything they tried to bury.

She finally whispered into her empty room, voice cracking:

"I miss you."

Across the country, Cole lay in the dark.

At the exact same moment, barely audible even to himself, he whispered.

"Ava..."

Neither heard the other.
But both felt the absence like a bruise.

A bruise that wasn't healing.
A bruise that was only getting deeper.

CHAPTER EIGHTEEN

Ava's alarm went off Monday morning—far too bright, far too cheerful for the way her chest felt like wet cement.

She dragged herself out of bed, made coffee on autopilot, and sat at her tiny desk—the same spot she'd worked from for years. The place that used to feel familiar. Warm.

It felt cold now.

Empty.
Wrong.

Her first Teams notification chimed.
Her stomach dropped.

Cole was already online.

She hovered over his name, staring at the tiny green dot next to it.

[Ava]: Don't click. Don't message. Don't look. Don't want.

She opened her first meeting.
She joined her first meeting.

Camera off.
Mic muted.

Her voice existed only when required.
The rest of her didn't.

She was careful to keep her name from bumping into his in any attendee list— skimming past it like touching it might burn her.

By noon, her coffee had gone untouched.
By five, her eyes burned. By nine, she crawled into bed still dressed, too tired to care.

Cole was unraveling, too.

He logged in early, hoping it would help— hoping that drowning his brain in work would numb everything else.

It didn't.

He opened his project dashboard.
Stared at it for a long moment.
Then he closed it again.

He made breakfast and forgot to eat it. He reread the same email three times without understanding it. He joined meetings and kept his camera off every time.

His team noticed.

Marcus messaged him.
Marcus: bro you good?
Marcus: you've been quiet.
Marcus: like... disturbingly quiet.
Marcus: what happened last week?

Cole set his phone face down.

He didn't answer.
He couldn't.

Every message felt like a bruise being poked. Every meeting felt like sitting on a fault line, waiting for something to crack.

Every time he heard Ava's name mentioned on a call, something inside him stuttered.

He kept his camera off.
He kept his comments short.
He kept his world small.

By Wednesday, she hadn't spoken a single sentence that wasn't work.

Her apartment felt hollow.
Her meals became afterthoughts.
Her energy leaked away by the hour.

During a meeting, she accidentally unmuted while sighing.

"Long week?" her coworker asked gently.

Ava forced a smile into her voice, flipping her camera on. "Oh, uh, yeah... something like that."

She turned her camera off again, ignoring the way her throat tightened.

Later, Becky messaged her.

Becky: girl are you alive?

Becky: u look like u got hit by a bus.
Becky: spill.
Becky: Ava.
Becky: something happened with Cole.
Becky: Didn't it?

Ava closed the chat.
Closed her laptop.
Closed off.

She went to bed early that night, but didn't sleep.

[Ava]: How do you miss someone you told yourself you couldn't have? How do you go backward? How do you pretend everything is normal when normal feels like a lie now?

By Friday, the cracks were obvious.

Cole missed a deadline for the first time in years. Ava turned in a workflow demo with errors she never made.

Their manager, Daniel, noticed.

He scheduled one-on-one meetings with them separately. Not knowing how connected their mistakes were.

"Ava," Daniel began, his voice kind in the way that made it sting more, "I wanted to check in. Your work has been... inconsistent."

She nodded lightly. "I know. I'm sorry. I've just been… tired."

"This isn't like you," he said. "You're one of our most dependable team members. Is something going on?"

[Ava]: A week of heartbreak, loneliness, pretending I'm fine, pretending he's not across the digital hallway from me, pretending nothing happened that changed everything.

"No," she lied softly. "Just burnout."

Daniel sighed. "I'm giving you a lighter load next week. But I need you back at full capacity soon, Alright?"

"Yeah," she whispered. "I know."

Daniel ended the call with Ava, jumping right into a meeting with Cole.

"Cole," Daniel said, exhaling, "your productivity took a nosedive this week."

Cole pinched the bridge of his nose. "I know. I'm sorry. It won't happen again."

"This isn't like you," Daniel repeated, a similar line he'd given Ava. "You're usually on top of everything. Is something going on?"

Cole hesitated.

For a moment, just one brief moment, he nearly said her name. But then he swallowed the truth.

"No," he said quietly. "Just an off week."

Daniel nodded slowly. "I need you sharp next week. Let me know if something changes."

Cole clicked out of the call and pressed both palms to his eyes.

[Cole]: I'm losing it. I'm actually losing it. And I can't tell anyone why.

Another week passed.
Then another.

Meetings blurred into each other.
Camera off became their new default.

Their names sat on the same call screens, inches apart in the participant list, but farther than ever.

Once, Ava unmuted to give an update, and Cole's chest tightened like he'd been hit.

Once, Cole made a joke in a sprint review, and Ava nearly cried because his voice sounded tired, and she knew that exhaustion too well.

Neither reached out.

Both wanted to.
Both didn't.

Their worlds had shrunk to small apartments and quiet nights and half-finished work, and every attempt to fix it just hurt worse.

The fog didn't lift.
The ache didn't fade.

They were doing exactly what they'd promised themselves they would.

Moving on.
Getting distance.
Being smart.

It wasn't working.
Not even a little.

CHAPTER NINETEEN

Ava didn't mean to disappear.

Not from work.
Not from her world.
Not from him.

But some moments don't wait for your life to be in order.

Her phone rang early Monday morning—far earlier than Brittany ever called—and the second Ava heard the trembling inhale on the other end, her whole body went cold.

"Aves?" Brittany's voice cracked. "It's—it's my mom. She had a heart attack. They're rushing her into surgery. I—I don't—I can't—"

Ava was already moving. "I'm coming."

"You don't have to—"

"Yes. I do."

She hung up, grabbed her suitcase, and threw in clothes without thinking, fingers shaking too hard to fold anything properly.

Brittany's mom, Mrs. Mills, had been a second mother to her since middle school. Soft cookies, warm hugs, and homemade soup when she was sick. The kind of woman who remembered birthdays and packed snacks for road trips. The type of woman who loved Ava unconditionally.

There was no universe where Ava didn't go.

She barely marked her calendar with PTO. Not adding any detail. She didn't message her boss. She didn't even pack her work laptop.

She booked a flight to New York and was out the door within twenty minutes.

[Ava]: She needs me. She needs me right now. Nothing else matters.

The hospital was a blur of white lights and frantic energy. The moment Ava spotted Brittany—folded into Zach's arms, sobbing— her chest cracked wide open.

Ava rushed forward, pulling Brittany into her arms.

"I'm here," she whispered, voice thick. "I've got you, Britt. I'm here."

The following hours dissolved into motion.

Paperwork.
Insurance.
Phone calls to family.

Getting consent forms signed that Brittany's father was too shaken to process.

Finding a vending machine that wasn't broken.

Coordinating with nurses.
Holding Brittany's hands.
Holding Zach up when he wavered.

Ava didn't eat.
Didn't sleep.
Didn't sit.

Every time she paused, even for a second, the ache in her chest throbbed.

[Ava]: He would've come with me. If things were different. He would've sat here. Held my hand. Told me to breathe.

She shoved it away each time.
There was no room for heartbreak.
Not today.

Meanwhile, Cole noticed by Tuesday.

Ava's Teams dot wasn't green.

Not yellow.
Just the gray X.
'Last active: two days ago.'

His stomach tightened.

Maybe she was sick.
Maybe she forgot to turn her status on.

Her calendar had no detail for PTO. Her calendar *always* had detail for PTO when she took it.

By Wednesday, he was hovering over her name like touching it might bring her back.

He typed: Hey. Everything okay?
He deleted it.

Typed again: Checking in. Haven't seen you online.
Deleted it.

Typed: I miss you.
Closed the window.

By Thursday morning, worry turned sharp.

He asked Becky.
He asked Marcus.
He checked her calendar again—still nothing.

And then his phone rang.
Zach.

Cole answered instantly. "Zach?"

"Maddox." Zach sounded dead on his feet. Frayed. "Britt's mom had a heart attack. They've been at the hospital nonstop. Ava came after Brittany called. She hasn't gone home in days. I—I don't know what to do."

Cole sat down hard. "Ava's in New York?"

"Yeah, she's been here all week."

Cole inhaled sharply. "Why didn't she tell me?"

Zach was quiet for a beat. "You two aren't talking?"

Cole closed his eyes, pain threading through him. "No," he said softly. "We're not."

[Cole]: Because we broke it. And I thought staying away would help us heal, not... whatever this is.

"Well," Zach breathed, "she needs people. Brittany needs people. Can you come? Just for the weekend."

Cole didn't hesitate. "I'm on my way."

He booked a flight within minutes.

Didn't care about cost, or layovers, or logistics.

Threw clothes into a duffel bag.
Left dishes in the sink.
Left his laptop open on the couch.

[Cole]: Whatever it takes. New job, new city, new everything—if it means being with her, I'll do it.

The thought was so clear, so bright, it stunned him.

He wasn't running from this.
Not anymore.

Ava stayed in New York as long as she could. Longer, honestly.

She hadn't slept more than an hour or two a night. She'd lived in hospital chairs and vending-machine snacks, holding Brittany together while Zach handled everything else.

She didn't check Teams. Didn't open her email. Didn't remember she had a job until her phone buzzed with an incoming call from Daniel.

She stepped into an empty hallway to answer it. "Hello?"

"Ava." Her manager's voice was clipped. Cold. "We need to talk."

Her stomach dropped. "I-I'm sorry. There's an emergency. I've been with family—"

"I'm aware," he said, "but disappearing without proper notice for nearly a week isn't acceptable. You missed two deadlines. You ignored every outreach. If you don't return immediately, we'll have to escalate this."

A write-up.
Maybe worse.

Ava closed her eyes, throat tight.

[Ava]: Not now. Please—not now.

"I'll fly home tonight," she whispered.

And she did.

Even though Brittany begged her to stay.
Even though she hated herself for leaving.
Even though her bones felt carved out from the inside.

She hugged Zach and Brittany tightly, promising she'd come back once things stabilized.

Then she ordered a rideshare to the airport. As the car pulled away, she looked back at the townhouse, aching.

[Ava]: I can't be here. I have to work. I can't lose that, too.

But it felt wrong.

Leaving.
Walking away.

Going back to a life that suddenly felt too small and too lonely. It felt like running.

Cole arrived only hours later.

Jaw tense.
Eyes bloodshot.

His heart was pounding so hard he felt a little sick. Zach opened the door with dark circles under his eyes. "Hey. You made it."

Cole stepped inside scanning the room. "Where is she?"

Zach's face shifted with sympathy and exhaustion. "Ava? She's gone."

Cole's heart kicked painfully. "Gone?"

"She flew home," Zach said quietly. "Her boss threatened a write-up. She didn't have a choice."

Cole stared at him like he hadn't heard correctly. "I missed her?" He pressed a fist briefly to his sternum, like he could hold himself together.

"Barely." Zach gave a tired, humorless half-laugh. "Honestly? You two probably passed each other on the highway."

Cole's breath left him in a slow, crushed exhale.

Of course, that's how this goes.

Just like before the wedding—missed flights, opposite weekends, bad timing, wrong timing, always-nearly-there-but-never-at-the-same-moment.

Always too close.
Never close enough.

It felt cruel now.
Personal.

Zach clapped his shoulder gently. "She wanted to stay. Really. But she was... wiped out, man. I've never seen her like that. She gave everything she had. For days."

Cole nodded, swallowing hard. "Yeah. That sounds like her."

He stepped inside fully, shoulders heavy.
Her jacket was still draped over a chair.
Her green Stanley on the counter.

Her phone charger was still plugged in, crooked and rushed.

She was everywhere.
And she wasn't.

Cole lowered himself onto the couch, elbows on his knees, hands rubbing together like he could warm the cold inside him.

He didn't know what the next days would bring. He didn't know if she wanted him in her life. He didn't know how to take one more step without her.

But he knew one thing with absolute certainty—Distance wasn't going to stop him.

He would cross any state.

Any job.
Any rule.
Any fear.
Any damn continent if he had to.

Whatever it took to stand beside her—He was going to do it. Even if he always arrived a little too late.

Again.

CHAPTER TWENTY

Cole stayed the entire weekend.

He made breakfast.
He drove Brittany's dad home.
He sat with Zach during long, silent hours in the waiting room.

He refilled water bottles, found chargers, made phone calls, did everything Ava would have done—except she wasn't there.

And Zach noticed.

Late Sunday night, with the house silent and Brittany finally sleeping after learning her mom would be released tomorrow, Zach looked over at him with red-rimmed, exhausted eyes. "You know she only left because she had to, right?" he said.

Cole swallowed. "Yeah."

"And she didn't tell you because she didn't want to drag you into the mess, and apparently things between you two..."

Cole looked down. "Too late for that."

Zach let out a soft huff of a laugh. "If you want my advice? Don't go back to Louisiana."

Cole raised his head.

"Go to her," Zach said. "She won't ask. But she needs someone. She needs you."

Cole didn't sleep at all after that.
By dawn, his flight to Seattle was booked.

He didn't text her.
Didn't warn her.
Didn't think it through.

He just went.

[Cole]: I'm done missing her by hours. I'm done pretending I don't care. I'm done being a coward.

Ava's Monday morning was the opposite of romantic.

She'd slept maybe four hours since returning from New York, and her eyes were puffy from crying in the shower. Breakfast was a stale granola bar. And her apartment felt too small, too quiet, and too dark.

She joined the project update meeting because she had to, not because she had the emotional capacity for human interaction.

Her manager was already mid-sentence when she unmuted.

"—so we'll need the new forms ready for Friday. Ava, you're up."

"Yep," she said, forcing professional energy into her voice. "I can take the lead on the form redesign and—"

Knock, knock.

She blinked.

"Oh—sorry, give me one second. Let me just—probably a delivery."

She kept speaking because the knock stopped. "So, the client wants updated CSS to match their new branding, so I'll adjust the styles after we finalize—"

Bang bang.

She jumped slightly at the urgent sound. Someone on the call raised an eyebrow.

"Everything alright, Ava?"

"Yeah—sorry—door's just... aggressive today." A weak laugh. God help her. "Move on, I can finish my update in a moment."

She tapped the space bar to mute—or so she thought.

Her mic stayed live.
Her camera stayed on.

Oblivious, Ava stood, straightened her sweatshirt, and crossed her tiny studio apartment toward the door.

The front door is in full view of meeting participants.

Someone whispered, "Is this... part of the agenda?"

Ava opened the door.
And froze.

Cole.

Breathless.
Hair wind tousled.

Chest rising and falling like he'd sprinted the last block. Eyes wide and terrified and relieved all at once.

Her knees went weak.

"Cole?" she whispered.

He didn't answer.
Didn't wait.

Didn't even look at the laptop behind her.

He stepped inside, closed the door with one hand, and with the other wrapped his arm around her waist and pulled her into him like he'd been drowning without her.

Before she could speak—before she could think—he kissed her.

A desperate, fierce, soul-deep kiss.

A kiss that tasted like airports and sleepless nights and the moment you finally stop running.

Ava gasped softly against his mouth, then melted into him, fingers curling into his jacket, kissing him back just as urgently.

Someone on her laptop gasped.

"Um—Ava—your camera—mic" as Daniel tried desperately to mute her, turn her camera off, something.

Becky's voice: "Is that Cole?"

Marcus' voice: "Holy shit."

Ava pulled back just enough to breathe, face flushed and stunned. "Cole—my meeting—my camera—everyone can see—"

He rested his forehead against hers, breath shaky. "I don't care."

"I do," she whispered, though she didn't stop holding him.

Behind her, her boss cleared his throat loudly.

"Ava," he said almost yelling through her laptop speakers, "You need to leave the meeting. We will discuss this later."

She shoved Cole away—gently, not actually wanting him to move—and sprinted back to her desk, slapping keys until the screen went black.

Mute finally activated.
Camera off.
Call abandoned.

She turned back to Cole, hands shaking. "You cannot just show up and kiss me in front of our entire team!"

He stood there, chest heaving, not even pretending to be sorry.

"I had to," he said.

"Had to?"

He took a step toward her.

"I thought something had happened to you," he said, voice raw. "You disappeared. You were gone, Ava. And I couldn't do another day pretending it didn't matter."

Her heart stuttered.

"Cole..."

He swallowed. "I flew to Louisiana," he said. "When the truth is, I should've flown here with you."

He shook his head slightly, voice rough. "I had it backwards. We had it backwards. Thought I was running toward something I needed..."

His gaze held hers.

"But I didn't understand the difference between the place I was going…"

"And the place I belonged." A small breath.

Ava's breath caught.

"I'm done being scared," he continued. "I'm done being hours too late. I'm done missing you. I'm here. If you want me gone, say it. But if you want me to stay—"

He reached for her hand.
"—I'm staying."

She stared up at him, heart pounding, throat closing, eyes burning.

"Cole," she whispered, "you just kissed me on camera."

He smiled softly. "Worth it."

A tiny, uncontrollable laugh escaped her.

She lunged into him, arms around his neck, kissing him again softer this time, but no less confident.

He held her tightly, lifting her slightly off the ground, breath warm against her cheek.

For the first time in weeks—maybe longer—Ava felt like she could breathe again.

Like something inside her had finally clicked back into place.

She wasn't sure what came next. What HR would say. What their team would say. What their lives would look like.

But for the first time since everything started...

She wanted to find out.

CHAPTER TWENTY-ONE

Ava stood rooted to the middle of her tiny studio apartment, heart thundering in her chest, staring at the closed laptop like it was a live grenade.

"Oh my God," she whispered to herself, pacing in a tiny, frantic circle. "I kissed a coworker. On camera. In a meeting. With my boss. And the director. And—oh God—maybe the CFO? I'm unemployed. I'm definitely unemployed."

Her hands flew to her face. She couldn't tell if she was overheating or freezing. Dread pooled low in her stomach, heavy and sharp.

[Ava]: Why am I like this? Why did I open the door? Why did he have to look like that when I opened the door? Why is my life a walking HR training video nobody asked for?

Behind her, Cole was still by the door where he'd closed it behind him. His chest rose and fell fast, his eyes wide, stunned, searching.

"Ava," he said softly.

She spun around. "Don't 'Ava' me. I'm having an out-of-body experience."

He lifted both hands, surrendering. "Fair."

"You just—you *can't* just show up and kiss me

like some kind of caffeinated movie hero—"

His lips twitched. "Movie hero?"

"Not the point."

He cleared his throat. "Okay. Sorry. Continue."

"—when our entire team was watching!"

A flicker of guilt crossed his face. "I genuinely forgot about the meeting."

"Of course you did," she muttered. "Why would you remember the concept of cameras? Or consequences?"

Ava took a sharp breath, forcing her brain to stop melting.

Cole swallowed. "Do you... want me to leave?"

Her chest contracted.
No part of her wanted him to go.

"No," she whispered. "Just... don't go."

He exhaled, relief visible, and stepped fully into the apartment—which meant taking exactly two steps before he ran out of space.

Her apartment was so small. Too small. Especially with Cole Maddox inside it.

Ava jumped when her phone vibrated violently on the counter.

Becky calling.

She groaned. "She probably thinks I eloped. Or got kidnapped. Or had a stroke."

Another buzz.
Twenty new messages—Becky

"Oh God."

Across the room, Cole's phone lit up too.
Marcus calling

Cole winced.
His phone buzzed again.

Twelve texts—Marcus: Bro, call me now.

He rubbed his forehead. "I'm gonna have to deal with that."

Ava tossed her hair into a messy knot. "We'll deal with it. But first... food. I need something solid before my soul leaves my body."

Cole moved to the kitchenette because his body needed something to do besides turn around and kiss her again.

Eggs.
Pan.
Stove.

Something simple.
Something grounding.

[Cole]: I kissed her on camera. I kissed her in front of the whole team. I would do it again.

He hated how true that last part was.

He cracked eggs into the pan. "Sit," he said gently. "You look like you're going to fall over."

Ava dropped onto a stool, head in her hands. "I can't believe this is happening."

He glanced over, softening. "I'm sorry if I made everything worse."

She lifted her head. "Cole. You flew across the country. For me."

His breath snagged.

She tilted her head, eyes warm in a way that unraveled him. "That doesn't make things worse."

He swallowed hard.
The pan sizzled.

[Cole]: God, I've missed her.

He set the plate in front of her. She looked at it like he'd crafted Michelin-star cuisine.

"You are a god," she muttered.

"They're just eggs."

"Do gods say things like that? No. They take the compliment."

He snorted.

"Eat," he said, and she did—like someone who'd been too stressed to feed herself all day.

His phone buzzed again.

Another message from Marcus:
Dude, did you make out with Ava in a meeting? What the hell.

Cole shut his phone face-down so hard it clacked.

Ava eyed him. "Everything okay?"

"No."

She nodded. "Same."

Her own phone lit up again.

Becky: Answer your phone you minx.
Becky: Who is he? Was it Cole?

Ava covered her face. "I can't deal with her right now."

"You should text her back."

"You should text Marcus."

They stared at each other.

"No," they both said.

After eating, Ava looked toward her laptop with the same expression someone might give a bomb made of bees.

Cole followed her gaze. "We should... deal with that."

"No," she said immediately.

He gave her a look.

She groaned. "Fine. But you're doing this with me."

"Obviously."

She sat at her desk—the only clear surface in the apartment—and opened the laptop like she was lifting a coffin lid.

Her inbox exploded.
Team.

"Are you okay?"

"Call me."

"Do we need to file an incident report?"

"Who is he???"

Her boss: Ava, let's discuss this when you're available.

HR: Please schedule time with us.

Her stomach hit the floor so hard she was surprised it didn't leave a dent.

Ava dropped her forehead to the desk. "I'm going to vomit."

"You're not," Cole murmured, rubbing her back once before catching himself and stepping away.

[Ava]: God, don't touch me right now unless you plan never to stop—because I won't survive the whiplash.

He pulled a chair beside her. "We write an email. Together."

She nodded.

Hands shaking. Cole sat so close she could feel the warmth of him, which was deeply unhelpful as she typed.

To: Manager, HR
CC: Cole Maddox
Subject: Follow-up on this morning's project meeting

Hi all,

I want to acknowledge the incident that occurred on camera earlier today. My coworker, Cole, stopped by my apartment unexpectedly because of a personal situation, and I stepped away from the meeting to answer the door without realizing that my camera and microphone were still active. The interaction was unplanned and unprofessional, and we apologize for the disruption this caused.

Cole and I are prepared to discuss appropriate next steps and ensure that this doesn't happen again.

Thank you for understanding,
Ava Harper
Cole Maddox

Ava stared at the message.

Cole read it slowly. "It's honest."

"It's humiliating."

"It's better than letting HR write their own version."

She sighed. "You're right."

She hit send.
The email whooshed away.

Ava curled into herself, knees to chest. "Okay. It's done. I can die now."

Cole rested his forearms on his knees, leaning toward her.

"Ava."

She looked at him.

"You're not alone in this."

Her chest squeezed.

"And whatever happens," he added softly, "I'm not going anywhere."

Her pulse jumped.

Against her will, against every ounce of self-preservation she had left—

She believed him.

CHAPTER TWENTY-TWO

Ava didn't even have time to breathe.

Her email had barely left her outbox—her finger still hovering above the trackpad—when her laptop chimed with a new notification.

She froze.

Cole straightened beside her like a soldier bracing for impact.

From: HR-General
Subject: URGENT: Meeting Request—Immediate
Time: 7 minutes from now

Participants: Ava Harper, Cole Maddox, Daniel Reyes (Manager), Christy Anders (HR Manager)

Ava stared. "Seven minutes?" like she'd been handed an execution time.

Cole exhaled slowly. "They didn't waste time."

[Ava]: Oh god. I'm not ready. I need water. I need an alternate identity. I need a time machine. Seven minutes? I'm going to pass out.

She forced her voice steady. "We should... join early?"

Cole nodded even though his jaw was locked tight.

[Cole]: I hate this. I hate that she's scared because of me. I should've waited. I should've asked. I should've—no. No. I'd do it again— every damn time.

He sat beside her at the breakfast bar. "Let's join on your laptop. Camera off."

"Camera is never going on again," Ava whispered.

They logged into the Teams meeting two minutes early.

The screen was blank.
No one else had joined.

Ava tapped her heel anxiously against the leg of her stool. "Maybe they'll just... give us a warning."

Cole didn't answer.
Because they both knew better.

Footsteps echoed outside her window.
A car horn blared in the distance.
A bird landed on her sill.

Everything felt too loud. Too sharp, like her senses were turned to max volume.

Then—

Daniel Reyes joined the meeting.

Ava sat up straight so fast she nearly knocked over her water glass.

Daniel's voice came through before his camera loaded. "Ava? Cole? We can stay audio-only if that's more comfortable."

Ava's stomach twisted. *Translation: We already saw more than enough of you this morning.*

"Audio is fine," Ava said, praying she sounded alive.

Cole nodded even though no one could see. "Same here."

Christy Anders joined the meeting.
HR's camera turned on immediately.

She was composed. Glasses. Professional ponytail. A small neutral smile that could mean anything.

"Thank you for joining so quickly," Christy said. "We'll address this promptly, so everyone understands expectations moving forward."

Ava swallowed. *I'm going to be fired, blacklisted, and living in a barn with goats by Friday.*

Daniel cleared his throat. "First, I want to acknowledge that this is uncomfortable. But we appreciate you both taking responsibility quickly."

Cole leaned slightly toward the mic. "It was my fault. I initiated—"

Christy held up a hand. "This is not a blame conversation. Regardless of who did what, there are some items we need to address before moving forward."

Ava blinked. *What does that mean? Why does that sound worse?*

Christy continued, folding her hands. "We need to confirm three things. One: Is this relationship consensual?"

Ava felt her pulse spike. *Relationship? Oh god, is it a relationship? Is it? Is it?*

Cole jumped in. "Yes. Completely."

Ava nodded. "Yes."

Two beats of silence.

Christy made a note. "Second: Is there a reporting chain, supervisory dynamic, or power imbalance?"

"No," Ava said immediately. "We're both Solutions Engineers."

"Equal level," Cole added. "No supervisory overlap."

"Good," Christy said.

Ava's shoulders loosened half an inch.

Christy continued, "Third: Are you, at this moment, formally entering a consensual workplace relationship?"

Ava felt like she'd swallowed a brick.

[Ava]: He kissed me less than an hour ago. We haven't even processed this privately. What does formally even mean? What if he says no? What if I say no? Are we... are we something?

Her heart thundered. She risked a glance at Cole.

His jaw was tight. Eyes forward. His fingers curled against the counter. Then—

Slowly, he nodded.

"Ava and I are... pursuing this seriously," he said, voice steady but soft. "So yes."

Ava inhaled sharply.

Her voice came out smaller. "We are? I—yes. Yeah. We are."

Christy nodded again and pulled up a digital form. "In that case, company policy requires a consensual relationship disclosure. I'll send it to both of you after this call."

Ava's heart was racing. *This is really happening. We just declared our feelings to HR before we even told each other.*

Daniel finally spoke again. "Now... about the meeting this morning."

Ava's stomach hit the floor.

[Ava]: Here it is, the guillotine.

"Ava," Daniel continued gently, "you forgot to mute and turn off your camera."

"I know," she whispered.

"And that's a serious lapse," he said. "You also interrupted the meeting during your update to handle something... unrelated to the meeting."

Ava blinked. *Can we get to the point? The punishment.*

Christy added, "It was unprofessional, but not malicious. We've seen the recording."

Ava covered her face. "Oh god."

Cole reached out under the counter and brushed her knee. Supporting.

Christy went on, "We will delete the recording from the server. It won't be used in training. It will not be referenced further. Ever."

Ava almost sagged with relief. She could breathe again, a shaky, uneven breath, but breath, nonetheless.

"We will issue both of you a written formal reminder about meeting etiquette and professionalism," Daniel said. "No suspension. Just a write-up."

Christy chimed in, "and additional training on professionalism in remote work settings. I will email you both the details."

Ava exhaled shakily. *Okay. I'm not being thrown into corporate exile.*

"And," Daniel added, "we recommend keeping future personal interactions off company calls."

Ava almost laughed. Half-hysterical. "Agreed."

Cole murmured, "Definitely agreed."

Christy closed the file. "We'll email the disclosure forms shortly. If you have questions, come to me directly. Otherwise, you're both free to go. Please take the rest of the day and recompose yourselves professionally."

The meeting ended.

Ava stared at the blank screen.

Then dropped her forehead onto the counter with a groan. "I'm going to die. Right here on my laminate countertop."

Cole rubbed her back gently. "You survived."

"I almost died."

"Same thing."

She turned slightly toward him. "You... told HR we were pursuing this seriously."

He paused.

Then nodded slowly. "Because I am."

Her breath caught. Her chest tightened, not with panic this time, but with something dangerously close to hope.

"I don't want to do this halfway, Ava," he said, voice quiet but confident. "Not after everything."

Her heart turned liquid.

"And you?" he asked, almost shy.

He nudged his knee with hers, a soft, deliberate touch. "Yeah. Seriously."

He smiled—soft, relieved, all the tension melting from his shoulders.

They looked at each other for one long, warm, terrifying moment. Then both their phones buzzed at the same time again.

Cole sighed dramatically. "Should we tell our friends?"

Ava smirked. "Or... hear them scream at us first?"

He leaned back. "Fair. We probably deserve it."

She laughed, light and finally free.
For the first time since the airport...
It felt like they might actually be okay.

CHAPTER TWENTY-THREE

They stared at their buzzing phones like they were grenades vibrating in judgment, threatening to blow up the situation.

Cole sighed. "Okay. Marcus first or Becky?"

Ava made a face. "Becky's already sent me twelve gifs. I think she's warming up."

"Marcus sent me a meme of a dumpster fire," Cole muttered.

Ava snorted. "Accurate."

They answered at the same time.

Ava typed: Alive. Busy. Will call later. Promise.

Cole typed: Not dead. Complicated. Will explain eventually.

Both phones buzzed again with the frantic energy of people who absolutely did not respect boundaries.

They ignored them.

Ava slid her phone face down. "I need... air."

Cole nodded. "I'll call Zach. He's probably pacing his house."

Cole rubbed the back of his neck, not out of uncertainty, but instinct, the way he always did when he needed to settle the noise in his head.

Ava caught the flicker of worry in his eyes before she grabbed her jacket and slipped outside into the cool Seattle drizzle. The street smelled like rain and damp pavement.

The cold drizzle hit her skin like the universe spritzing her with a "Get it together" spray bottle, and her head finally felt clear enough to think.

[Ava]: This is insane. Cole showed up. HR knows. My team knows. My boss knows. This is the most aggressively unhinged Monday the universe has ever gifted me.

Her stomach twisted. Every good thing felt like it came with a hidden trapdoor, and she could never tell when she was about to fall through.

She dialed Brittany.

The call barely rang before Brittany answered, breathless. "Ava Harper start talking!

Ava winced. "Hi?"

"No hi. Zach told me Maddox changed his flight to see you?"

Ava groaned. "Britt. Please. One crisis at a time."

Brittany inhaled sharply. "Okay. I'm calm. Start from the beginning. No, wait. Start from the kiss. Actually, no. Start from when he showed up at your door like a man who committed a felony of the heart."

As Brittany rambled, a knot formed in Ava's throat. She wanted to laugh it off, but all she could think was: What if I already ruined this?

Ava leaned against a brick wall and closed her eyes. "He just... showed up at my door. He didn't even text. And how do you know about the kiss?"

"That is either incredibly romantic," Brittany said, "or a man completely unhinged with love. Becky called me."

Ava's heart stuttered. *Love. Oh god.* The word hit like a live wire. Too big. Too bright. Too close to everything she secretly wanted and was terrified to reach for.

"We had a meeting," Ava said quietly. "HR. Daniel. Christy. They know."

"What did they do? I'll fight them."

"Nothing. Just paperwork. A warning. A future training."

Brittany exhaled loudly. "Thank god."

Ava hesitated. "Britt... do you think this is actually possible? Cole and I?"

"Yes," Brittany said instantly. "But you're overthinking it already. Stop spiraling. Enjoy it."

[Ava]: I want to. I really, really want to.

God, she wanted to. She didn't know how to stop waiting for the ground to shift beneath her.

"I'm scared," she admitted softly. "Not of him. Of wanting something so badly it breaks me if it goes wrong."

Ava pressed her fingers to her forehead. "He's staying for the week."

"What?!"

"We're both working remote. And he wants to... be here."

Brittany squealed so loudly Ava had to pull the phone away from her ear. "Oh my God. I knew it. I knew he was in love with you."

Ava whispered, "Britt—stop saying that."

"But he is."

Ava didn't respond.

Because she didn't trust herself not to hope.

Inside the apartment, Cole paced as soon as Ava left.

He dialed Zach.

Zach answered on the first ring. "Dude. What the hell?"

Cole winced. "Hi to you too."

"You kissed Ava in front of your entire team.

"I panicked!"

"You panicked in the direction of her mouth."

Cole dragged a hand through his hair. "I didn't think. I just went with it."

Zach groaned. "I don't know whether to be impressed or terrified."

"Both," Cole muttered.

A pause.

Then Zach's voice softened. "You okay?"

Cole swallowed. "Yeah. It's just... real now."

"You like her," Zach said gently.

"Yeah," Cole whispered. "I do."

"You're staying there all week?"

"Yeah."

"You scared?"

[Cole]: Terrified. Completely. Utterly—like I jumped off a cliff expecting wings.

"A little," Cole admitted. "This isn't just flirting anymore."

"Nope," Zach said. "It's grown-up feelings. Welcome to the best kind of hell."

Cole laughed despite himself. "Thanks."

"Don't screw it up," Zach added. "She's important to Brittany and me. And obviously to you."

Cole nodded slowly. "I won't."

He hoped.
God, he hoped.

Ava returned twenty minutes later to find Cole sitting at her breakfast bar with his phone, shoulders tense.

He looked up.

"You okay?" he asked.

Ava nodded. "Are you?"

"Zach threatened my life. So yeah."

She laughed softly and slipped off her jacket. "Okay. Ground rules."

Cole perked up. "Ground rules?"

She held up one finger. "This apartment has one bed."

"I noticed."

"And you're not sleeping on the floor."

Cole's mouth curved. "Okay."

"But you're also not sleeping with me."

His eyebrows shot up. "Okay."

"So... a wall of pillows. For safety."

He smirked. "Sure. If that helps."

Ava glared at him. "It will."

He cleared his throat. "Second rule?"

Ava blinked. "There's no second rule. I just panicked."

Cole chuckled. Something warm fluttered inside her chest.

CHAPTER TWENTY-FOUR

The week settled into a strange, beautiful rhythm.

In the mornings, Cole made coffee. In the afternoons, they worked—Ava at her desk, Cole at the breakfast bar, hunched over her ancient spare laptop that wheezed when he typed too fast.

"Harper," he said on Tuesday, tapping the trackpad, "this computer has seen some stuff."

"It works!"

"Barely."

"That's rude."

"You deserve better technology."

"You deserve an attitude adjustment."

He smirked. "Make me."

She threw a cereal bar at his head.
He caught it and took a bite.

They shopped for groceries and argued about cereal brands. They cooked badly and burned half the pasta.

They bumped into each other in the tiny kitchen approximately twenty-three times a day.

They kept brushing hands, always by accident, never unnoticed. They kept looking away too quickly.

And every night, they climbed into Ava's bed, stayed carefully on their own sides, and stared at the ceiling like two people praying for sleep that never came. Every shift of the mattress felt like a temptation.

Don't reach for him. Don't touch her. Don't be stupid. Don't fall harder.

They were both doing terribly.

Thursday night, Cole said, "Let me take you out. Properly."

Ava blinked. "Like... a date?"

He hesitated, but only for a second.

"Yes," he said softly. "A real one."

Her heart flipped. "Okay."

He smiled, slow and warm. "There's a diner near Pike Place. Nothing fancy. But it's us."

[Ava]: Us. God.

Ava could've melted into the floor.

They walked there at sunset, his hand brushing hers every few steps, neither brave enough to grab the other's.

The diner was tiny, warm, and glowing with yellow light. They sat in a corner booth and ate burgers and fries, talking about everything and nothing.

Ava teased him about the aquarium date.

Cole teased her about her folder structure on Teams.

They laughed so loud that the waitress smiled every time she passed.

At one point, Cole reached across the table and took her hand without thinking.

Ava's breath hitched. Her entire body went still, like the world was waiting for her reaction. His thumb brushed her knuckles.

"Hey," he murmured.

She swallowed. "Hey."

The world felt... good.

Real.
Possible.

But Sunday came.
Too fast. Too heavy.

Ava stood at her apartment door while Cole zipped his suitcase.

He kept pausing. Stopping and starting again.

Neither of them spoke.

Finally, Cole exhaled shakily. "I hate this. Leaving you feels wrong."

Ava nodded, hugging her arms around herself. "Me too."

"I'll be back," he said quickly. "I just need to wrap things up. Work. My lease. My life there."

Ava nodded again. *Don't cry. Don't make this harder. Don't cling.*

Cole stepped close.

He cupped her cheek with one hand, slow and careful. "Ava Harper," he whispered, "don't doubt us. Not for a second."

Her throat tightened. "I'm trying."

"I know."

She rose on her toes and kissed him—soft, trembling, lingering.

He kissed her back with both hands in her hair like he didn't want to let go.

Then he did.
He stepped back.

Grabbed his suitcase.
Opened the door.

Looked at her one last time with eyes so warm she nearly broke.

"I'll call when I land."

She nodded.
He left.

The door clicked shut.
Ava pressed her forehead to the wood.

[Ava]: Please don't let this be the part where everything falls apart. Please come back. Please choose me.

Down on the street, she heard the rideshare honk. And then he was gone.

CHAPTER TWENTY-FIVE

Working remotely used to be Ava Harper's favorite thing. Now it was emotional torture with Wi-Fi.

Three weeks of watching Cole Maddox pixelated and out of reach. Three weeks of shared screens, shared documents, shared smiles, they pretended not to notice. Three weeks of coworkers trying and failing not to comment on the shift between them.

Screens could show his face, but never the way he looked at her. And she missed that most.

During Thursday's project sync, Jordan leaned forward, squinting at his monitor.

"Ava, are you frozen or just... staring?"

Ava jolted so hard her headset tangled in her hair. Cole pressed his fist to his mouth in the corner of the screen, shoulders shaking.

Heat slammed into her face so fast she was surprised the webcam didn't fog.

Later in the team group chat:

Maya: y'all... the tension is *visible*.
HR Christy: Friendly reminder: workplace chat is for work conversations only.
Jordan: sorry shutting up now.

Cole: this is awkward.

Ava's face went hot enough to power Seattle's electrical grid.

Every night, she replayed their week together: the shared breakfasts, the working side by side, the way he'd sit at her tiny breakfast bar with her old, wheezing laptop.

He'd tap the lid gently and say, "Don't die, buddy. We believed in you yesterday. Believe today."

She'd snort every time. She missed that stupid voice more than she wanted to admit.

And now? They were back to two screens, states apart, and a constant hum of nerves in her chest.

Every night they had a virtual dinner.

Every night, they talked on the phone until one of them fell asleep.

Every night, Ava wondered.

[Ava]: *How long can I do this? How long before long-distance crushes the fantasy? How long before he realizes I'm not worth uprooting his life for?*

Wanting him was terrifying; believing he could really want her back felt downright impossible.

She vented to Brittany during their almost daily calls.

"What if he changes his mind?" Ava whispered as she shoved laundry into the dryer.

"Girl," Brittany said flatly, "he is literally moving states for you. Moving. States."

Ava winced. "I know."

"You don't act like you know."

Ava flopped onto her bed. "I'm scared, okay?"

Britt's voice softened. "He chose you. That's real."

Ava didn't trust her voice long enough to answer. This wasn't a fling. This was a choice that could reshape both their lives, and that terrified her.

Three weeks of chaos.
Real adult chaos.

Cancel the lease.
Sell half his furniture.
Pack boxes.

Research Seattle neighborhoods.

Schedule movers that cost more than his first car. Work full-time. Sleep... occasionally.

He'd missed his work laptop the week he stayed with Ava, using her backup machine instead, an ancient device that whined like it needed emotional support. Now that he was home, he clung to his real laptop like a lifeline.

But even familiar routines felt wrong without her.

He'd make coffee and wish he could hand her a mug. He'd open Teams and wish she were across the tiny breakfast bar again. He'd close his eyes at night and feel the space where she used to sleep curled beside him, warm and soft and very, very real.

He tried to talk to his family.
It didn't go well.

His sister, Emery, crossed her arms. "You're leaving Louisiana for a *girl*?"

"Not 'a girl.' Ava, the woman I'm in love with," he corrected. "And we're not teenagers anymore."

"You barely know her!"

"I know enough."

Emery huffed. "You're abandoning everyone."

Cole exhaled through his nose. "We live in the same city and haven't had dinner in four months."

"That's not the point."

"It's literally the point."

His parents weren't angry, just stunned. No one in the Maddox line had left Louisiana in… ever. They acted like he'd announced he was joining a Mars colony.

But worst of all? The quiet doubt in his own head. *What if I am making a mistake? What if I can't make Ava happy? What if I am repeating my pattern—falling hard, too hard, and messing it up?*

He confessed it to Zach one night.

"I'm terrified," Cole admitted, pacing his half-empty living room. "I've already been the idiot who let something at work implode. I cannot risk that happening with Ava. Not when she matters this much."

"… what happened with Bree was a blip. Seriously. You two barely dated. Half the drama came from the office rumor mill, not you."

Cole scrubbed a hand over his face but said nothing.

Zach continued, gentler this time.

"Bree wasn't love, man. She was timing, convenience, and maybe a little boredom. It fizzled fast because it was never meant to last."

Another pause.
Then:

"Ava is not Bree. She actually means something to you. And you've never meant anything like this to anyone before."

Cole sank onto the arm of his couch, shoulders tight. Zach's voice softened even more.

"You're not repeating the past. Ava is different. And that's exactly why you won't screw this up."

Cole didn't say it out loud, but he hoped Zach was right.

One gray afternoon, Ava shut her laptop and walked along the waterfront, needing air.

Needing clarity.

Needing anything that wasn't overthinking.

She called Brittany.

"Talk to me," Brittany demanded immediately. "You sound like you're in your existential crisis voice."

Ava kicked a pebble across the sidewalk. "What if this doesn't work? What if I hurt him? Or he hurts me? Or everything feels different once he's here?"

Brittany snorted. "Welcome to relationships. Population: everyone losing their minds."

Ava let out a strangled laugh.

"Seriously," Brittany said, "you can't think your way around feelings. You have to live them."

Easy for her to say. She wasn't the one falling in love with her coworker-turned-wedding-week-turned-long-distance situationship.

And beneath all of it lived another fear she hadn't admitted aloud.

[Ava]: What if he gets here... and realizes I'm not worth the move?

Cole hung up after talking with Zach and stared around his half-packed apartment.

He hated it.
He hated the silence.
He hated the distance.

He hated waking up without Ava beside him.

He pulled out his phone and opened the apartment listing he liked in Seattle. He could picture her there cooking with him, laughing, curled up on the couch with her feet in his lap.

[Cole]: I need to get there, I need to be where she is.

He booked movers for the two weeks out when his new apartment would be ready.

Then he booked a flight.

By the end of the third week, Ava snapped.

Not in a dramatic way.
Not in a crying-on-the-bathroom-floor way.

More in a: *If I don't see him soon, I'm going to go insane* way.

She bought a ticket to Louisiana.
Brittany's response was instant:

Brittany: Go get your man.
Brittany: And wear something cute.
Brittany: But not too cute.
Brittany: Actually, wear whatever you want ok bye.

Ava had never packed so fast in her life.

Plane.
Rental car.

That soft flutter of reckless hope in her stomach.

[Ava]: He's going to be so surprised. He's going to kiss me the moment he sees me. This is going to be perfect.

She repeated that to herself the entire drive from the airport.

By the time she pulled up to his apartment building, her hands were shaking.

She climbed the stairs.
Took a breath.

Knocked.
No answer.

She knocked again.
Still nothing.

[Ava]: Maybe he's sleeping? Maybe he's in the shower? Maybe—

She raised her hand to knock a third time—

The door swung open.
And Ava froze.

Standing in front of her was a red-haired stranger, gorgeous and half-dressed.

Tall.
Model-level gorgeous.

Barely dressed in a silky robe that hung open far more than it closed.

Ava's stomach dropped through the floor.

"Oh," the woman said, blinking at her. "Can I help you?"

Ava opened her mouth.
Nothing came out.

Her chest tightened.
Her ears rang.

Her heart fell apart in the space of a single exhale.

The woman leaned against the doorframe, brow lifted. "Are you looking for Cole?"

Ava couldn't speak.
Her throat locked.

Her lungs forgot how to function.
Her heartbeat thudded so loud it was all she could hear.

The woman's smile tilted sympathetically like she *knew* exactly what Ava was thinking and didn't feel remotely threatened by it.

"He should be back soon," the redhead added casually, tightening the sash of her barely tied robe. "He stepped out to get *us* breakfast."

Us.

Ava felt the word like a slap.

Her stomach lurched, something hot and nauseating rushing up into her chest.

She didn't correct her.
Didn't demand an explanation.

Didn't say *I'm his girlfriend*. Didn't say *I flew halfway across the country for him*. Didn't say *He told me he loved me in a way that wasn't love but also absolutely was*.

She couldn't say anything.
She just backed away.

One step.
Then another.

Then she turned and walked—fast—down the hallway.

By the time she reached the parking lot, she was running.

Her hands shook so violently that she fumbled the keys twice before she finally yanked open the rental car door and collapsed inside.

The moment she shut the door, the tears came hard and uncontrollable—ugly, silent, body-shaking.

[Ava]: How could I be so stupid? How could I think he meant it? He said he was scared of messing things up. Maybe he already had. Perhaps I was a week-long vacation. A pretty fantasy. A mistake.

Her breath hitched. She pressed the heel of her palm to her mouth, trying not to sob loud enough for someone to hear.

Her phone felt heavy in her hand.
She hit call.

Brittany answered on the first ring.

"Finally! Did he sweep you off your feet? Did he—Ava? Ava? Babe? What's wrong?"

Ava tried to breathe, but it came out as a broken gasp.

"There was—" She wiped her face, but the tears kept coming. "A woman."

Silence. Then—

"A *what*?"

"A woman," Ava whispered. "In his apartment. Barely dressed. She said he went to get breakfast for *them*."

On the other end of the call, chaos erupted.

Brittany shrieked, "Zachary! Zach get in here!" A muffled thud, a door slamming.

Ava pressed her hand over her mouth, trying to steady her breathing.

Brittany came back on the line, voice shaking with anger and heartbreak for her. "Ava... baby... I'm so sorry. I'm so, so sorry."

Ava let out a slight, broken sound. "I shouldn't have come. I shouldn't have surprised him. I just—I thought—"

"No." Brittany's voice sharpened instantly. "No, absolutely not. You did nothing wrong."

In the background, she shouted again, voice cracking: "Call him! Call Maddox! He screwed up, Zach! He broke her heart! He's your friend—call him!"

A heavy exhale from Zach followed, low and pained: "I'll call him."

Ava shut her eyes, tears blurring everything. "I just want to go home."

"Then come home," Brittany said softly, fiercely. "Right now. Don't wait, don't explain, don't do anything. Just get on a plane or drive—just come home to me, okay?"

Ava nodded even though Brittany couldn't see her. "Okay."

"And Aves?" Brittany added, voice thick but controlled. "Whatever this is... whatever happened... you're not doing this alone. We've got you. Always."

Ava let out a trembling breath. "Thank you."

She hung up before she could completely fall apart.

Cole walked down the cracked Louisiana sidewalk with two breakfast sandwiches balanced on one arm and iced coffees sweating through the cardboard tray in the other. The air was thick, warm, humid home. Or what used to feel like home.

[Cole]: *Just a couple of weeks more.*

Just fourteen days and he'd be back in Seattle for good. He couldn't wait to tell Ava. Couldn't wait to see her face when he said the words out loud: *It's official, I'm moving to you.*

His phone vibrated in his pocket.
Zach.

Cole smiled and shifted the coffees to answer. "Hey man, I—"

"What did you do?"

Cole blinked, stopping mid-step. "Uh... excuse me?"

"You heard me!" Zach roared. "What. Did. You. Do."

Cole stopped walking completely. "Zach, what the hell are you talking ab—"

"You need to listen to me right now," Zach snapped, breath sharp, furious, and afraid at the same time. "Ava showed up at your apartment. Some half-naked woman answered the door."

Cole felt the blood drain from his face.

"No. No Zach, that's—"

"She's crying her eyes out!" Zach shouted over him. "She thinks you cheated! She thinks you were sleeping around while trying to move across the damn country for her! Were you?!"

"Zach—Zach, stop—listen—" Cole's voice cracked as he started walking again, fast. "It's not what she thinks. That's my sister. My sister. Emery. She stopped by last night and—"

"Then why did she answer your door looking like she just rolled out of your bed?"

Cole broke into a jog. "Because she drank too much and crashed on my couch! That's it! Zach, I swear on everything—nothing is going on. It's Emery."

There was a stunned silence.

Then Zach exhaled hard. "Jesus Christ."

"Where is Ava?" Cole asked, turning the corner of his building so sharply he nearly slipped.

"You're not gonna like this," Zach muttered.

"Tell me."

"She's already back in her rental car," Zach said quietly. "She's getting ready to head toward the airport."

Cole's chest tightened painfully. He reached the bottom steps of his apartment building and sprinted up them two at a time.

"Zach—I would *never* hurt her." His voice shook. "You know that. You know that."

"I do," Zach said firmly. "But she didn't stick around to get the story. She's heartbroken, man. You don't know what she went through with...you don't know, man."

Cole fumbled the key into the lock with shaking hands, flung the door open—and froze.

Emery stood there in his robe, half awake, hair wild, mascara smudged, blinking at him like he was the one doing something wrong.

"Where's the emergency?" she mumbled. "What's-"

Cole held up a hand, breathless, panicked, not even looking at her. He put the phone back to his ear.

"Zach."

"Yeah."

"I'm going after her."

"Good," Zach said. "Run."

Cole didn't even hang up properly.

The phone slipped into his pocket.
Breakfast hit the counter.
He spun and bolted back out the door.

Down the stairs. Across the lot. Past two startled neighbors.

Running harder than he had in years.
His only thought, repeatedly.

[Cole]: I'm not losing her. Not again. Not this time.

Her hands shook on the steering wheel.

[Ava]: I trusted him. I trusted him more than anyone since—She swallowed, throat tight.

Since Nathan. The man who had said all the right words, made all the right promises, and still managed to break her in the ugliest way possible.

She blinked hard, vision blurring.

"No. Not again," she whispered to herself. "I won't be that stupid twice."

She put the car in drive.

But before she could even hit the gas—Bang. Bang. Bang.

Ava flinched as someone slammed their hand against her window.

Her heart lurched.

[Ava]: No. No. Cole.

Running in front of the car.

Breathless.
Wild-eyed.
Panic etched into every line of his face.

She froze, hands hovering over the wheel.

He held both palms up, like he was approaching a terrified animal.

"Ava," he mouthed, "Please."

She couldn't roll down the window. If she did—If she let him speak—If she heard his voice—

She knew she would break.

He cheated, she told herself. *He lied. Men like him always lie. Don't fall for it again.*

She tightened her grip on the wheel, jaw trembling.

Cole stepped closer, breath fogging the glass.

"Just—listen—please," he said, voice muffled through the window.

Ava shook her head. Hard.
He looked gutted.

He knocked again, softer this time. "Ava. It's not what you think."

[Ava]: Of course, he said that. They all said that. Every man caught in a lie had the same script.

She reached for the gear shift.

Cole's hand slammed flat against the window. "Don't go."

Her breath hitched painfully.
His chest felt like it was collapsing.

Ava wouldn't roll the window down. Wouldn't look at him. Her eyes were everywhere except his, wild and devastated, as if she were trying to outrun the moment.

"Ava, please," he begged, stepping into her path before she could pull forward. "Just give me ten seconds. Ten. That's all."

She shook her head again, lips pressed together so tightly they turned white.

Cole's voice broke.

"It's Emery," he said desperately, pointing back toward the building. "She's my sister. My sister. She, she drank too much last night and crashed on the couch. That's all."

Ava's eyes flickered—just for a second—but they didn't soften.

She whispered, barely audible through the glass, "Move, Cole."

"No." He planted himself in place. "I'm not letting you leave thinking I would ever— ever—do that to you."

He could feel the panic clawing up his throat.

He'd lost her once.
For weeks.

And it had nearly unmade him.
He wasn't losing her now.
He wasn't.

"I love you," he blurted before he could stop himself. "Ava, I—"

Ava jerked like he'd struck her.

Her eyes filled instantly with fear, heartbreak, disbelief swirling into something that punched him in the ribs.

She put the car in park, just long enough to drop her forehead against the steering wheel.

Then she whispered one broken sentence he barely heard.

"You sound just like him."

Cole's stomach dropped. "Like who?"

She looked up with tears streaking her face.

"My ex," she choked out. "The last time I believed someone the way I believed you, I walked in on *this exact scene.* And I'm not doing it again. I can't."

Cole staggered back a step.

"Ava, no, God, no—I'm not him."

He reached for the door handle—She hit the lock button faster.

He flinched like it physically hurt.

"I'm not lying to you," he said helplessly. "Please. Please let me explain."

But she was already wiping her face, already shifting into drive again.

[Cole]: She's leaving. Oh God. She's going to leave.

"Ava, Ava, look at me—"

She looked at him.
Just once.
A single, shattering second.

Then she whispered.
"I can't do this, Cole."

And the car started rolling.

From the second-floor window, Emery watched the rental car inch forward with a cold, satisfied little smirk.

"Good," she murmured. "Maybe now he'll stay where he belongs."

"No—No—Ava!"

He ran after the car, palms slamming onto the trunk as she accelerated.

"Ava! Stop!"

But she didn't.
Couldn't.
Wouldn't.

Cole slowed, finally collapsing to his knees in the middle of the parking lot, hands braced on the asphalt, chest heaving like he'd just lost air, lost gravity, lost everything.

He whispered her name once more, voice breaking on it.

"Ava..."

She was already gone.

CHAPTER TWENTY-SIX

The airport was cold in a way that sank straight into her bones.

Ava stood at the Delta counter gripping her suitcase handle so tightly her knuckles ached. Her heartbeat thudded behind her ribs, too fast, too loud—like her body hadn't caught up to the fact that she'd already left.

"Any flight to New York," she said, voice thin. "Tonight. Tomorrow. Doesn't matter what airport. I'll take anything."

The agent tapped quickly, eyes kind but unapologetic.

"Everything's booked for the next forty-eight hours. Summer traffic, plus unexpected weather on the East Coast." She winced. "I'm so sorry."

Ava swallowed hard.
Of course, that would happen.
Why would anything go right today?

"Okay," she whispered. "Standby? Anything on standby?"

"I can put you on three lists," the agent offered. "But... they don't look promising."

Ava nodded because she didn't have the strength not to.

Her phone buzzed for the fifteenth time in ten minutes.

Brittany: Where r u? Call me. Now
Brittany: I need to know you are safe.
Missed call from: Cole Maddox.

Ava stared at that last one until the screen blurred. She should call him. She wanted to call him. But wanting wasn't enough.

She turned her phone face down on the counter and forced a breath.

"I'll just... sit near the gate," she said numbly.

The agent gave her a sympathetic look. "If something opens, I'll call you immediately."

"Thank you."

Ava stepped away on autopilot, weaving through crowds until she found an empty chair facing the window. Outside, planes lifted into the sky one after another.

Each one leaving.
Each one escaping.
Each one was going somewhere she wasn't.

Each one lifting off toward a place where things weren't so impossibly broken.

She curled her knees toward her chest, resting her forehead against them.

[Ava]: I shouldn't have come here. What was I thinking? Showing up unannounced like some romance movie idiot? Stupid, stupid.

Because deep down, she'd rather run than be left behind again.

Her breath hitched.

Then her phone buzzed again.
She didn't pick it up.

Didn't look.
Didn't move.
She closed her eyes.

And for the first time since she left his parking lot—A sob clawed its way out of her throat.

Running had felt like safety. Now it just felt like a loss.

The apartment door slammed open hard enough to rattle the frame. The sound echoed through the empty apartment, far louder than he meant it to.

"What the hell is wrong with you?" Cole's voice hit the walls hard, louder, sharper, the Louisiana in it breaking through like he'd forgotten to hold it back.

Emery jumped, nearly spilling her coffee. She was now in jeans and a tank top, hair pulled into a messy ponytail like she hadn't just answered the door in lingerie thirty minutes ago.

"Oh, please," she scoffed. "If this is about the girl—"

"Her name is Ava!" Cole roared, his accent thickening around the words like it came straight from his gut. "And you knew that was her at the door!"

Emery crossed her arms. "She didn't introduce herself."

Cole's voice cracked with fury. "Emery, don't play dumb. You *knew*. You've been snooping in my messages since I announced my move." The vowels snapped sharper than usual, his Southern edge slicing through the fury he couldn't contain.

Her mouth twitched.
Guilty.

So goddamn guilty.

"She's moving you across the country," Emery muttered bitterly. "What did you expect me to do? Celebrate?"

"Yes!" Cole exploded. "Or, and this is wild—just Not sabotage my life!"

She blinked, startled by the sheer volume of his anger.

Cole ran a hand through his hair, pacing. "She came to surprise me. She thought—God, Emery, she thought I was cheating on her."

"That's not my fault," Emery snapped. "If she's that insecure—"

"No." He pointed sharply at her. "You do not get to talk about her like that."

Something flickered in her expression—hurt, jealousy, fear.

"You're my younger brother," she said stiffly. "You're supposed to be here. With us. With family. Not running off to Seattle for some girl you barely know."

"I know her," Cole shot back. "Better than anyone. She mattered before I ever saw her in person."

Emery's jaw tightened. "Well, she's gone now."

The words stabbed him.

Cole's breath left his lungs. "Because of you," he whispered.

That landed.
Hard.

Emery looked away, swallowing. "You're throwing away your entire life."

"No," he said, calmer now. "I'm choosing it."

A beat.

Then Emery grabbed her purse with a sharp movement.

"Fine. Screw it. If you're going to ruin everything, do it without me."

She stormed toward the door.

"And Emery?"

She paused.

Cole's voice dropped to a deadly calm.

"If she never speaks to me again... if I lose her over this... I will never forgive you."

Emery flinched.
Actually flinched.

Then she slammed the door and left.

Cole stood in the sudden silence, breathing hard. Then he sprinted for his keys. He didn't care if he had to run every light.

He was going to find Ava.

He wasn't letting her leave the state, thinking he'd betrayed her.

Not now.
Not today.
Not ever.

"Ava," he whispered into the empty room, grabbing his jacket.

"Please still be here."

He ran.
Her phone buzzed again.

Cole Maddox—seven missed calls and three voicemails.

Text: *Ava, please. Let me explain.*

One More text: *I'm coming to the airport. Don't leave.*

Another text: *Ava, I swear to you it wasn't what you think.*

And finally: *Please wait for me.*

Ava covered her mouth, shaking.

"No," she whispered. "Don't come here. Don't—please—don't make this harder."

But her heart—

Her heart thudded painfully at the thought of him running through terminals looking for her.

She wiped her face, trying to breathe.

Trying to think.
Trying to be rational.

But nothing felt rational.

Nothing felt steady.
Nothing felt safe.

Ava didn't know how long she sat there.

Minutes. Hours. Time didn't feel real in airports, the lights were always the same brightness, the announcements always the same tone, the people always moving while she couldn't seem to.

"Passenger on standby for Delta Flight 317 to New York, Ava Harper—please come to the podium."

Her head snapped up. For a moment, she thought she'd imagined it.

Another announcement crackled overhead, clearer this time:

"Last call for standby passenger Ava Harper for Flight 317, departing for New York. Please approach the gate."

Her breath caught.

Her legs moved before her brain did, shaky and unsteady, pulling her suitcase behind her like it weighed as much as the hurt sitting in her chest.

The gate agent smiled softly when Ava reached the desk, like she already knew the shape of the story.

"You're in luck. We had one no-show," she said, printing a boarding pass with quick, practiced movements. "If you still want to travel, I can get you on. They're closing the door in two minutes."

Ava swallowed hard.

[Ava]: If you still want to travel.

Did she
Did she want distance? Space? Safety?

Or did she want him to burst through the terminal shouting her name like some impossible movie miracle?

[Ava]: Don't think. Don't hope. Don't break.

"I'll take it," Ava whispered.

The agent handed over the ticket, and Ava walked down the jet bridge on shaking legs. No dramatic music. No last-minute footsteps behind her. Just the low hum of the engines warming and the ache in her chest that pulsed with every step.

[Ava]: This is the right thing. This is what you need. This is what keeps you safe.

She repeated the lies until she almost believed them.

Almost.

She found her seat, 18A, by the window, and buckled herself in. Her phone buzzed repeatedly in her pocket, but she didn't dare take it out. If she looked... if she heard his voice...

She might run off this plane and straight into the kind of heartbreak she'd never come back from.

A tear broke free.
She swiped it away angrily.

The cabin door shut with a heavy clunk.
Too late.

The engines growled louder as the plane pushed back from the gate.

Ava finally pulled out her phone to text Brittany her flight details.

Messages lit up the screen.

Cole: Ava, please. Let me explain. I swear to you it wasn't what you think. Please wait for me. I'm coming to the airport.

Her heart dropped. She covered her mouth to stop the sound that clawed up her throat.

He was coming here. He was running toward her while she was being taxied away from him.

"Please stop," she whispered to the phone, tears blurring the screen. "Please don't make this harder."

The plane turned.
Accelerated.
Lifted.

Ava closed her eyes against the ache. *He's going to get here, and I'll be gone. He'll think I didn't care.*

Another tear slid down.

"This is what I have to do," she whispered to the window.

But it didn't feel like strength.
It felt like a loss.

Cole's foot slammed down on the gas pedal so hard the engine protested.

Traffic in had never felt so suffocating, so slow. He wove through lanes with the kind of focused panic that made drivers honk and flip him off.

He didn't care.

He'd explain. He'd beg. He'd tell her everything he should've told her days, weeks, *years* ago.

He pictured her at the terminal, curled in some hard plastic seat, crying alone because of something his sister had done.

He tasted bile.

"Hold on, Ava," he muttered, knuckles white around the wheel. "I'm coming. I'm right here. Just, hold on."

He skidded into long-term parking crookedly, barely turned the ignition off before he bolted toward the sliding doors.

Inside, the airport was buzzing kids with snacks, businessmen in suits, families arguing over boarding passes. Cole shoved past them, ignoring the annoyed looks.

He reached the departures board, heart pounding.

Atlanta.
Dallas Fort Worth.
Seattle.

He scanned the board again, pulse spiking.

SEA 712 STATUS: Departed

His stomach dropped.

"Shit, shit, no—"

He sprinted toward security, weaving between stanchions like a man possessed.

"If you're traveling alone, sir, please stay in line," a TSA agent barked.

Cole ignored him.

"You can't cut, hey! You can't cut!"

Cole threw his shoes into a bin, yanked off his jacket, and emptied his pockets with shaking hands.

[Cole]: Move.

His hands shook so badly that he dropped his wallet.

He nearly screamed.

Finally, he got through the scanner and sprinted toward the gate.

People stared as he ran past, breath ragged, heart shredding itself with every step.

He saw the gate in the distance.

"Wait!" he shouted, voice cracking. "Is the flight to Seattle still here? Please—"

The gate agent looked up, startled.

"I'm sorry, sir," she said gently. "Boarding is complete. The aircraft door is closed."

Cole stumbled.

"It—she—did you see a girl? Dark hair, sweatshirt, crying—Ava Harper—did you—"

The agent softened. "I am sorry, I can't give you that information sir."

His breath punched out of him.

Too late.
He was too late.
Again.

He turned away, pressing both hands to the back of his neck as the world tilted.

[Cole]: *She thinks I cheated on her. She thinks I lied. She thinks I didn't choose her. And now she's gone.*

His phone buzzed in his hand.

Zach.

He answered with a broken, "Please tell me she's still here."

"Brittany got a text" Zach said quietly. "She's in the air"

A hollow, painful laugh escaped him. "Of course she is."

He sank down onto a chair in the gate area.

"What do I do?" he whispered. "Because I swear to God, Zach, if she never speaks to me again—"

"You text her," Zach said. "Once. Tell her the truth. And then give her space."

Cole squeezed his eyes shut.

"I can't lose her."

"You won't," Zach said. "Not if she knows you love her."

Love.

The word crashed into him like a truck.

He'd thought it for months. Years. But now, it felt like the only lifeline he had left.

Cole typed with trembling fingers.

Cole: I know I'm the last person you want to hear from. But I need you to know this. I did not cheat on you. The woman you saw was my sister. I should have told you more about her. That's on me. I love you, Ava. I'll explain everything when you're ready. No pressure. No rush. I'm here.

He hit send.

And the tiny "delivered" nearly broke him.

No reply came.
He didn't expect one.

He leaned forward, elbows on his knees, staring at the floor as the gate agent announced that Flight 712 had left.

It wasn't over.
It hurt like it was.

Ava's plane leveled out at thirty thousand feet. Clouds stretched endlessly below like soft, indifferent mountains.

A flight attendant passed by offering pretzels.

Ava didn't take any.

She just stared out the window, eyes puffy, face blotchy, heart cracked wide open.

Her phone, now in airplane mode, rested in her lap.

She knew the messages were waiting. She knew his words were sitting there like a heartbeat she'd chosen to silence.

"I'm sorry," she whispered again, forehead pressing to the cool plastic.

Somewhere below, Cole was standing in an airport full of people, believing he'd lost her.

And for the first time since she boarded, she let herself cry freely.

For him.
For her.
For whatever they had been.

For whatever they still could be—if the world wasn't so impossibly complicated.

She didn't know what would happen next.

But the plane kept moving forward.

And for now, that would have to be enough.

CHAPTER TWENTY-SEVEN

By the time the plane landed at LaGuardia, Ava felt like she'd been scraped out and poured back in wrong.

Her body moved on autopilot, unbuckle, stand, shuffle forward with the rest of the passengers—while her brain replayed the last two hours in a relentless loop.

Cole at security.
Cole at the gate.
Cole getting there three minutes too late.

The look she imagined on his face at that gate haunted her worse than anything else.

[Ava]: Stop. Don't picture it. Don't—

"Passengers, welcome to New York," the flight attendant chirped over the intercom. "Local time is 11:42 p.m."

New York.
Not Seattle.

Not her apartment, but *home*.
Whatever that meant anymore.

She followed the crowd up the jet bridge, through the bright, too-loud terminal, down toward baggage claim even though she only had a carry-on. Her legs felt like they belonged to someone else.

Her phone buzzed as soon as it found a signal again. Dozens of notifications flooded her screen.

She ignored every one of them except the contact labeled Brittany.

Brittany: We're at arrivals. Text when you're near the doors. Also, I brought snacks and emotional support.

Ava's throat tightened. Of course, Brittany came through. She always did. And that hurt in a way Ava didn't expect.

She typed back with clumsy fingers.

Ava: Walking out now.

The sliding doors parted with a blast of cold New York air and exhaust. Brittany was already half out of the car, waving like a maniac.

"There she is!" she yelled, like Ava was a rock star and not a shattered human being in an airport hoodie.

Ava barely managed a weak wave.

Brittany closed the distance herself, crashing into Ava with a hug so fierce it knocked the breath out of her.

Ava clung back, suitcase handle digging into her palm.

"Okay," Brittany murmured into her hair. "Okay. I've got you."

The words cracked something open.

Ava pressed her face into Brittany's shoulder and, for a second, let herself stop being brave. She clung harder because, for the first time all day, someone was holding her together.

It hurt.
But it also helped.

Zach appeared a moment later, grabbing her suitcase with the gentle efficiency of someone who'd done this before.

"Hey, Aves," he said softly. "We're glad you're here."

She nodded against Brittany's shoulder, unable to trust her voice.

They bundled her into the backseat. Brittany climbed in beside her instead of up front, curling one leg under herself, basically forming a human armrest around Ava.

It felt like high school again: late-night drives, bad breakups, and Brittany's mom's minivan.

Except this time, Ava had more to lose.

"Okay," Brittany said once they were back on the freeway, voice soft but determined. "Here's the plan. Mom insisted we come straight to her place. She already made the guest bed and pulled out the good blankets."

Ava's chest clenched.

"She doesn't have to—"

"Don't even try it," Brittany cut in. "You know she lives for this. Emotional triage is her love language."

Zach snorted quietly from the driver's seat.

"She really does," he agreed. "She put on a pot of tea at, like, eleven-thirty at night."

Ava let out a shaky laugh that sounded more like a hiccup.

"Of course she did."

[Ava]: Of course she did. Because when your heart broke in this family, there were protocols in place.

And step one was always: Go to Brittany's mom.

The minute they pulled into the familiar driveway, Ava's knees nearly buckled.

Everything looked the same.

The porch light.
The crooked flowerpot.
The little ceramic frog that had been sitting by the steps since Brittany was twelve.

The front door flew open before they even made it up the walk.

"Sweetheart," Mrs. Mills said, eyes already shining. "Oh, honey."

Ava didn't remember moving, just suddenly being wrapped in arms that smelled like vanilla candles and laundry detergent.

"Hey, Mom," Brittany sniffled, which was ridiculous because Brittany wasn't the one falling apart.

Ava let herself be steered inside, shoes off, coat off, and suitcase abandoned somewhere near the hall table.

Mrs. Mills cupped her cheeks gently. "Do you want tea, or bed, or a good cry first?"

The answer was yes.

"Yes," Ava croaked.

"Bed first," Mrs. Mills decided. "Tea can wait. Feelings can come in the morning. Come on, baby girl."

She led Ava down the hallway to the same guest room that had seen the aftermath of every major heartbreak since her freshman year of high school.

The sheets were already turned down.
The bedside lamp glowed warm and soft.
A box of tissues sat within arm's reach.

Of course it does.

Ava crawled into bed without bothering to change clothes. She just... folded.

Mrs. Mills lay down beside her on top of the blanket, like she'd done almost a decade ago when Nathan had smashed Ava's heart into tiny, jagged pieces.

Back then, it had felt like the end of the world. This somehow felt worse.

"What happened, honey?" Mrs. Mills asked quietly, stroking her hair back.

Ava stared at the opposite wall. She could see it like a movie she didn't want to watch again.

The parking lot.
Emery's bare legs.
Cole's face.

Her own.

She tried to speak.
Her throat closed.

"Later," Brittany said softly from the doorway, saving her. "Mom, let her sleep."

Mrs. Mills looked torn.
But she nodded.

"We'll be here when you're ready," she murmured into Ava's hair. "You are not alone, do you hear me?"

A hot tear slipped down Ava's cheek.

"I hear you," she whispered.

Because that was the worst part of all of this: With Cole, she had never felt alone. Now she did.

They dimmed the light.

Brittany kissed her forehead like a big sister instead of a best friend.

"We love you," she said. "You're safe."

The door clicked shut.

Ava stared at the faint golden strip of light beneath it until her eyes finally slid closed.

Sleep didn't fix anything. But it let her stop thinking for a while.

Which was enough.

Morning came with the rude enthusiasm of Brittany's mom cracking the door and whisper-shouting, "I made waffles."

Ava's eyes burned, gritty and swollen. She had no idea what time it was. Her body had no idea what state it was in.

"Mm," she managed.

"You have a meeting at nine," Brittany murmured from the edge of the bed, where she'd curled up sometime between two a.m. and dawn. "We figured we'd let you sleep as long as possible."

Ava's stomach lurched.

[Ava]: Right. Work.

HR friendly, camera-on, "I'm totally fine" work.

"Where's my laptop?" she croaked.

"In the living room. We set up a little office for you," Brittany said.

[Ava]: Office.

It turned out to be the dining table, angled so the background looked like a generic wall and not a shrine to Brittany's childhood trophies.

Ava sat down with her coffee, opened her laptop, and pretended her heart wasn't currently dust.

Her inbox was a disaster.

Her status dot had bounced between on, off, in-flight, and nonexistent.

There were pings from Becky.
From Jordan.
From Daniel.

From HR, which made her stomach actively try to leave her body.

No time for that.

She joined the daily standup with fingers that still shook.

Her camera blinked on.
Her own face stared back at her, puffy-eyed, pale, pretending.

"Morning, Ava," Daniel said, voice extra gentle in a way she hated. "Everything alright?"

[Ava]: No. Not even a little.

"Yeah," she lied. "Sorry, travel. I'm working remotely from my friends for a few weeks."

"Good," he said. "We'll try not to overload you."

She gave a tight smile.

Names flickered on the screen as people chimed in with updates.

Her eyes kept darting to the participants' list.

There he was.
Cole Maddox.

Camera off.
Muted.
Just a name.

Just a tiny gray circle that made her chest twist.

[Ava]: You can leave the meeting. You can drop. You can—

"Ava?" Daniel prompted. "Status on the vendor portal forms?"

She cleared her throat. "Right, sorry. I... can have the redesigns ready by Friday. I'll work with... whoever's available on the logic update."

She didn't say Cole.
She couldn't.

"Alright," Daniel said. "We'll shuffle resources as needed."

The meeting moved on.

Ava stared at the screen and decided she'd been circling since the plane. She was not doing this for the next month.

She was not going to sit in meetings with him, pretending nothing happened, feeling her insides scrape raw every time he cleared his throat.

The second the standup ended, she opened a new email.

To: Daniel Reyes
Subject: Team Adjustment Request

Her fingers hovered.
Then typed.

Hi Daniel,

I'm reaching out to request a temporary team adjustment or project reassignment through the next quarter. There are some personal circumstances that are making it difficult for me to be effective on projects where I'm closely paired with Cole, and I want to make sure I'm still delivering at the level the team needs.

I'm happy to discuss details privately, but the short version is I think a little distance would help me stay focused and productive.

I really value this role and our team, and I want to do what's best for all of us.

Thanks for understanding,
Ava

She read it twice.

It was vague, professional, and honest enough without inviting follow-up questions she wasn't ready to answer.

Her cursor hovered over Send.

[Ava]: Do it. You have to be able to breathe.

She clicked.

The whoosh sounded too loud in the quiet dining room.

From the kitchen, Brittany called, "You want strawberries or chocolate chips on the second waffle?"

"Both," Ava croaked.

[Ava]: Emotional damage justified emotional carbs.

They sat at the table after breakfast, Ava with her laptop, Brittany reviewing her wedding photos, Mrs. Mills wandering through occasionally to replenish coffee and ask if Ava needed another blanket, another snack, another anything.

It should've been cozy.
Normal.

It almost was.

Brittany watched Ava over her mug as she finished another email.

"Hey," she said gently. "We... kind of need to talk about logistics."

Ava tensed.

"I know," she said. "But can we not talk about *him*?"

Brittany nodded immediately, eyes soft.

"Absolutely. Zero Cole. This is a Cole free zone. No Maddox mentions. This is a Maddox vacuum."

"Thanks," Ava whispered.

She didn't have the capacity to rehash it. To hear "I'm sure it's a misunderstanding," or "he loves you, you know," or anything that sounded remotely like hope.

Hope hurt worse than anything.

Brittany flipped open a little notebook. "Okay. Here's what we were thinking. You stay here for a week or two, decompress, work from the dining table, eat Mom's food, and let her passive-aggressively spoil you into emotional submission. Then, if you want, you can crash with us the rest of the month. Or bounce back and forth if you prefer."

Ava blinked. "The rest of the month?" Brittany shrugged. "You said you needed time. Time doesn't happen in three business days."

Time.
Space.
A month.

The idea made Ava's chest squeeze with both relief and guilt.

"What about my apartment?" she said. "My plants? My—"

"Already texted Nick," Brittany said. "he's dying to sublet your place for a few weeks. Wants a 'Seattle workcation.' His words, not mine."

Ava's heart stuttered.

"Nick would stay there?"

"Yep. He'll water your plants, and send you pictures so you don't spiral about someone else using your coffee mug."

"I wouldn't spiral," Ava muttered.

Brittany raised an eyebrow.

Ava groaned. "Okay, I might spiral. A little."

"So, text him," Brittany said, sliding her phone over like a prescription. "One month. Starting, say... tomorrow?"

Nick was always willing to travel, and if it helped Ava, who was basically his little sister, he was there. Nick was Brittany's older brother and had been there through their entire friendship, a protector, a shield. He had even been there during the Nathan incident.

One month.
Four weeks.

Thirty days where she didn't have to accidentally see him at her favorite coffee shop. Where she didn't have to walk past the restaurant where they'd had their first official date. Where Seattle could stop feeling haunted for just a second.

"Okay," she said softly. "One month."

She typed the message with a tiny, fragile spark of control.

Ava: Random question: would you still be down to sublet my place for a bit? Thinking of staying in New York for a month to work remotely.

Nick answered in under thirty seconds.

Nick: Would. I'm already packing. Also, I

am very mad at whoever made you want to leave town this hard, but I will water your succulents and your feelings.

Ava smiled for the first time that day. It hurt, but in a good way.

"Nick's in," she said.

"Of course he is," Brittany replied.

Mrs. Mills wandered by, setting a hand on Ava's shoulder.

"That's settled then," she said in her soft, no-arguments voice. "You belong to us for the next month."

A lump formed in Ava's throat.

"Thank you," she whispered.

She meant.

Thank you for making space.
Thank you for not asking too many questions.
Thank you for giving me time when all I know how to do is rush. Brittany squeezed her hand under the table.

"No more talking about it today," Ava said, swallowing hard. "Please? I just... I need a day where he isn't the only thing in my head."

"Done," Brittany said instantly. "We will only

discuss important matters, like which takeout has the best dumplings and whether we can convince Mom to buy the good ice cream."

"Rude," Mrs. Mills called from the kitchen. "I already bought the good ice cream."

Ava let out a real, honest laugh.
It didn't fix anything.

But it made breathing easier.
For now, that was enough.

On the other side of the country, Cole stared at an empty suitcase.

Clothes lay in folded stacks on the bed, T-shirts, jeans, the one button-down Ava once complimented in a call, and he never quite got rid of.

He had a list on his phone of utilities to cancel. A lease-end checklist. A move-in checklist for the Seattle apartment he'd put a deposit on weeks ago.

He hadn't canceled it.
He hadn't even seriously considered it.

"Because you're stubborn," he muttered to himself.

His laptop chimed with a new email.
He almost didn't look.

Then he saw the subject line.
Team Adjustment Request, Ava Harper.

His chest tightened.

He sat down slowly, like the floor might shift under him.

The email was brief.
Professional.
Careful.

He could almost hear her voice in it, trying to sound fine.

...difficult for me to be effective on projects where I'm closely paired with Cole...

He flinched.

[Cole]: *Of course, she asked for a transfer. What did you think that she'd keep collaborating with you as if nothing had happened? That she'd laugh it off.*

He pressed his thumb and forefinger to his eyes until he saw sparks.

He let his hands fall.

If distance was what she needed to be okay— even if it meant losing the one bright part of every workday—then he wasn't going to stand in the way.

His phone buzzed.

A text from Zach.

Zach: How are you holding up, man?
Cole stared at the question for a moment.
Cole: Packing. Got the email about her requesting a team transfer.
Zach: You going to fight it?

Cole's fingers hovered.
Then he typed.

Cole: No. I told her I'd explain when she's ready. She's clearly not. I'm not going to push.

Dots appeared, disappeared. He could almost hear Zach's sigh.

Zach: Brittany says she's... breathing. That's about as much as we can ask for today.

Something in his chest unclenched by a millimeter.

She was breathing.
It wasn't enough.
But it was something.

Cole: Thanks. For being there.
Zach: Always.
Cole huffed out a laugh that didn't feel entirely hollow.
Cole: Already signed a lease. The place is big enough for...well. It's big.

He didn't type the rest.

Big enough for two people.
Big enough for another toothbrush.
Big enough for the future he'd thought he was walking into with her.

He shoved the phone into his pocket and started loading clothes into the suitcase.

One folded piece at a time.

He packed the hoodie that Ava once said looked soft. The mug Brittany had sent him with "World's Most Patient Best Man" etched on the side.

The stupid souvenir keychain he'd bought in the airport on his way back from their week together, because it had a tiny cartoon of the city where they'd first met.

He'd been so sure, then.
So ready.

He still was, in a way.
Just... on mute.

Give her space, he told himself again. *Move. Work. Breathe. Let her heal.*

He snapped the suitcase shut.

Took one last look around the room that didn't feel like home anymore.

"See you on the other side," he muttered to the walls.

Then he turned off the light and walked out.

Two weeks later, Ava sat cross-legged on Brittany and Zach's couch, laptop balanced on a pillow, a half-eaten slice of pizza on the coffee table.

She'd fallen into a rhythm.
Mornings at the dining table.

Afternoons walking the neighborhood with Brittany, the cold New York air biting her cheeks awake.

Evenings curled up with Mrs. Mills and whatever crime show or baking competition was on.

She hadn't spoken to Cole.
Not once.

She'd seen his name in calendars, on meeting invites, in the occasional reply-all email.

But no direct pings.
No calls.
No pressure.

He was keeping his promise.
It should have made it easier.

Sometimes it did.
Sometimes it made her chest ache worse.

"Okay," Brittany announced one night, dropping onto the couch with dramatic flair. "New topic, so we don't spiral: have you decided if you're going back to Seattle at the end of the month or if you're staying and becoming our permanent roommate?"

Ava smiled faintly. "Tempting."

"Just think about it," Brittany said. "We could start a commune. You, me, Zach, Mom down the block, a dog—"

"You're not stealing my hypothetical dog," Zach called from the kitchen.

Brittany stuck her tongue out in his general direction. "I gave you a whole human wife. I get visitation rights on the dog."

Ava laughed, the sound softer than it used to be but real.

"I'll go back," she said quietly. "Eventually."

"You don't have to decide today," Brittany replied. "All you have to do is show up to work tomorrow, eat actual food, and maybe brush your hair."

"That's a lot," Ava muttered. Brittany bumped her shoulder. "You can handle it."

Ava believed her.
Mostly.

Her phone buzzed on the coffee table. For a second, her heart tripped, expecting his name.

It wasn't.

Nick had sent three pictures of Ava's apartment, sunlight streaming through the windows, plants thriving, a mug of coffee on the bookshelf.

Nick: Your space says hi. Also, I rearranged your kitchen cabinets, but only a little. Please don't fire me.

Ava smiled, the tug in her chest different this time.

Home was still there.
Waiting.
So was he.

Somewhere in Seattle, probably standing in the middle of a too-big apartment, wondering if he'd just made the biggest mistake of his life.

Or the first right one.
Ava didn't know yet.

She wasn't ready to find out.
Not today.

"Movie?" Brittany asked, already reaching for the remote.

"Yeah," Ava said, closing her laptop. "Something with zero romance." Brittany scoffed. "So, like, two options total?"

"Exactly."

Mrs. Mills walked in with a bowl of popcorn big enough to feed a small town.

"Girls," she said. "I bring you carbohydrates and emotional amnesia."

Ava tucked herself between them on the couch.

No one mentioned Cole.
No one mentioned Seattle.

For ninety minutes, there were only bad special effects, shared eye rolls, and the feeling of being held together by other people's hands.

She still missed him.

She probably always would, in some shape or form.

But for the first time since she got off the plane, she believed something simple and small:

She was going to be okay.
Eventually.

Even if she didn't know what that would look like yet.

CHAPTER TWENTY-EIGHT

Cole didn't mean to end up on Ava's doorstep.

Not exactly.
He meant to unpack.
He meant to shower.

He meant to sleep for more than twenty minutes without dreaming of airport terminals and her face crumpling in a way he would never forgive himself for.

But his new apartment still smelled like fresh paint and disappointment.

Her name was still the first thing he saw every time he opened his messages.

And the silence was louder than anything.

So, at 11:47 p.m., after two and a half whiskeys, a six-pack, and approximately nine different internal speeches about giving her space, Cole found himself in a rideshare pulling up in front of Ava's Seattle building.

The lights in her apartment were on.
His chest stuttered.

[Cole]: Maybe—God, maybe she wanted to talk. Maybe she realized—Stop. Don't do that to yourself.

He climbed the stairs anyway.

Every step felt like a stupid, reckless hope he couldn't quite kill.

If she were there...

He didn't know what he'd say. He didn't know how he'd say it. But he'd take even ten seconds of seeing her face, knowing she was okay, breathing the same air—

He reached her door.

Swallowed hard.
Lifted his hand.
Knocked.

Three long raps.

He waited.
His pulse hammered.

The deadbolt slid.
The door opened.

And—

It wasn't Ava.
At all.

A tall, broad-shouldered guy with messy blonde hair and a half-eaten bag of Cheetos stared back at him.

"What," the guy said, blinking at Cole like he was a raccoon that learned how to knock, "is happening right now?"

Cole froze.

The guy blinked again.
Then frowned.

"Why do you look like someone just curb-stomped your soul? Did the Mariners lose? Is this a baseball thing?"

Cole's entire brain flatlined.
For a full three seconds, he didn't speak.
Couldn't.

Because this was Ava's door.
And this man was in her doorway.

In her apartment.
In her space.

"Oh God," Cole whispered, voice breaking. "Oh, shit. You're—"

"Nick," the guy said, pointing at himself with two orange-dusted fingers. "Brittany's brother."

Cole blinked.
Then blinked again as the pieces scrambled into place.

[Cole]: Nick. Brittany's brother. In Ava's apartment.

Not...Not Ava with another guy. Not Emery's nightmare scenario playing out in real time.

Just—

A house-sitter.
A male house-sitter.
Standing where Cole hoped she'd be.

Emotion crashed through him so fast he swayed.

Nick's eyes widened. "Dude, are you gonna pass out? Should I catch you? Is that a thing I'm supposed to offer?"

Cole braced a hand on the doorframe.

"I'm sorry, I just—I thought—"

"You thought I was Ava?" Nick asked.

"No," Cole said.

Then winced.

"...Yes."

Nick squinted at him. "Are you drunk?"

"Yes," Cole answered honestly.

Nick nodded sagely. "That explains the vibe."

Cole scrubbed a hand over his face. "She's not here."

"Nope."

"She's still in New York."

"Correct."

"She didn't come home."

"Nope."

Cole closed his eyes.

For a second, his throat tightened so badly he couldn't swallow.

Nick's voice softened, not much, but enough to notice.

"You want to... come inside?" he offered awkwardly. "Because you look like you're about to either cry or barf on the welcome mat, and Ava will kill me if her mat gets ruined again."

Cole shook his head. "No, I shouldn't. I told her I'd give her space."

Nick raised an eyebrow. "But instead, you drove across the city at midnight to stare dramatically at her door like a rom-com cryptid?"

Cole blinked.

"...Yes."

Nick shoved the bag of Cheetos under his arm and leaned on the doorframe.

"Alright," he said, "I have two options for you. One: I call Brittany and tell her you showed up looking like the human embodiment of emotional damage. Or two: you tell me what the hell is going on so I know whether I should let you walk back to your ride in this condition."

Cole looked up, startled. "You'd... tell them?"

"If I think you're a danger to yourself?" Nick shrugged. "Absolutely. I'm the responsible sibling. Jury's still out on Britt."

Cole almost laughed.
Almost.

Instead, he rubbed his face again. "I'm not going to do anything stupid. I just needed to see if she was okay."

Nick studied him for a long second.

"You really loved her, huh?"

Cole's breath hitched.

"I still do," he said quietly.

Nick let out a low whistle. "Damn."

He stepped back inside a little, hand still on the door.

"She's not here, man. She's with Brittany and Zach. She's safe. She's sleeping, probably."

Cole nodded, jaw tight.
Nick hesitated.

Then: "If it helps, I've seen her cry before. Like, after that Nathan guy wrecked her life. This is different. That was heartbreak. From what Brittany has told me this is... scared."

Cole's chest cracked.

"Yeah," he said hoarsely. "I know."

"So, give her time," Nick said. "Don't show up drunk at her apartment again, though. That part's weird."

Cole huffed out a miserable, tiny laugh.

"Yeah. Okay."

Nick softened just enough to show he wasn't actually a jerk.

"You want a water before you go?"

"No," Cole said. "I should go to sleep. Or... attempt to."

Nick nodded and pulled the door mostly shut.

Then paused.

"Hey, man?"

Cole looked back.

"For what it's worth..." Nick shrugged. "I don't think she's done with you."

Cole's breath stopped.

"What?"

"I said... I'm not repeating that," Nick grumbled. "Britt would lecture me for interfering, and Zach would give me that disappointed dad look he does. Don't give up yet."

The door shut entirely.

Cole stood there for a full minute, staring at the wood grain, feeling every ounce of whiskey leave his bloodstream in a crashing wave of clarity and regret.

Then he turned.
Walked back down the hall.
Out into the cold Seattle night.

He didn't feel better.

But he didn't feel alone either.

Somewhere on the other side of the country, Ava was breathing.

And somewhere inside him, something small and stubborn whispered.

Not over.
Not yet.

CHAPTER TWENTY-NINE

By week three, Brittany hit her limit.

Ava should've seen it coming. There had been signs.

The way Brittany kept opening her mouth like she was about to say something, and then stuffing more popcorn in instead. The way Zach would clear his throat and then abruptly ask about spreadsheets. The way Mrs. Mills had started bringing Ava tea with a side of "whenever you're ready to talk about it, I have opinions."

But Ava had made one rule.
No Cole.

No rehashing.
No analyzing.
No, "he loves you, you know."

Just waffles, crime shows, and pretending her life hadn't gone nuclear.

So, Brittany tried. She really did.

Until Tuesday afternoon, when she walked into the dining room, took one look at Ava hunched over her laptop with dead eyes on a sprint board, and announced.

"Okay. I can't do this anymore. We're talking about it."

Ava glanced up, exhausted. "About what?"

Brittany gave her a flat look.

"You know what."

Ava's stomach clenched. "Britt—"

"Nope," Brittany said, pulling out the chair next to her and sitting down with the determination of someone about to stage an intervention. "You don't get to permanently 'nope' this. You got two and a half weeks of emotional silence. I am cashing in my best friend tokens."

Ava's throat went tight. "I don't have anything new to say."

"Cool," Brittany said. "Then shut up and let me talk."

That actually startled a laugh out of Ava. Britt's expression gentled.

"You're not on social media," she said. "Which is usually one of your most charming qualities. However, in this situation, it's a problem."

Ava blinked. "I fail to see how not posting pictures of my lunch is a problem."

"Because," Brittany said, reaching into her hoodie pocket for her phone, "you have no way of fact-checking your trauma brain. Fortunately, I do."

Alarm prickled at the base of Ava's neck.

"Britt..."

"I'm not going to show you anything that hurts you," Brittany said softly. "I'm going to show you something that might... un-hurt you. A little."

She unlocked her phone, fingers moving with the practiced speed of someone who had been deep-diving accounts for days.

"First: you remember you told me her name was Emery?"

Ava's heart stuttered.

"Yeah," she whispered. Brittany nodded and spun the phone around, scooting her chair closer so their shoulders touched.

"Okay. Exhibit A."

On the screen was a profile.

Emery Maddox.

A smiling picture: sundress, sunglasses, a beach behind her.

Ava's stomach dipped. Brittany flicked to a photo.

A group shot at a restaurant, balloons, cake, and people crowded around a long table. Emery. A middle-aged man, Ava recognized from a framed photo on Cole's side table. Another guy with Cole's eyes. And—

Cole.

Standing slightly off to the side, one arm slung around Emery's shoulders, the other holding a huge margarita. He was laughing at something out of frame, head tilted, his features soft in a way that made Ava's chest ache.

Underneath the caption.

@emerymaddox: Birthday dinner with the chaos crew wouldn't trade my baby brother or this loud ass family for anything #MaddoxMess.

Ava stared at the words.

"Baby brother," Brittany read quietly. "And if you scroll—"

She flicked down.
More posts.

So proud of my genius little brother @ colemaddox for his promotion! Family game night at Dad's. Cole cheated at charades, again.

When your brother stops by for the weekend to assemble IKEA furniture for you.

Each one was a punch and a salve at the same time. Ava swallowed around the lump in her throat.

"He could've faked this," she whispered, then immediately hated herself for saying it. Brittany turned and leveled her with a look.

"Babe. This account goes back ten years. There are pictures of them as teenagers. There are braces. There is unfortunate haircuts. There's a phase where Cole clearly thought leather bracelets were a personality."

Ava winced. "Oh God."

"Exactly," Brittany said. "You cannot fake that much cringe."

Ava's eyes burned.

She wanted to be angry. To cling to it. To hold onto the one clean storyline, she'd had: he betrayed me, I left, end of story.

But the evidence on the screen was annoyingly, stubbornly clear.

Sister.
Family.

Not a lingerie-wearing random woman he'd chosen over her.

She pressed her fingers to her temples.

"He still didn't tell me," she whispered. "About... any of this."

"I know," Brittany said gently. "He should have. He should've told you about Emery. He should've had better boundaries with her. He should have been ten times more explicit that there was a half-dressed person in his apartment for reasons that were not 'cheating.'"

Ava let out a miserable half-laugh.

"But lying and not explaining," Brittany continued, "are two different things. And you've been punishing him like he did the first one when everything I see here says the second."

Ava slumped back in her chair.
The dining room blurred a little.

Their interaction that day replayed in her head—his voice wrecked, the text he'd sent from the airport.

The woman you saw was my sister. I love you. I'll explain everything when you're ready.

Her chest squeezed.

"What if I go back," she whispered, "and I believe him, and then something else happens? What if I'm just... setting myself up all over again?" Brittany sighed.

"I can't promise you nothing bad will ever happen again," she said. "I wish I could. But here's what I *can* tell you. I've seen him after you left. I've seen the way he stayed at the hospital with Zach. I've seen the way he moved states."

She poked Ava's arm with the phone.

"And I've seen his stupid, lovesick face in a hundred tagged photos he didn't know anyone would ever use as evidence. That man is gone for you."

Ava's eyes filled.

"I don't know how to trust myself anymore," she admitted. "I knew Nathan was bad for me and stayed anyway. I told myself I was being smart with Cole, and I still panicked and ran. What if my gut is just... broken?"

Brittany's voice softened. "Then don't trust your gut alone. Trust the people who love you. Me. Zach. Mom. Nick. We are telling you: this is not Nathan."

A tear slid down Ava's cheek.
She wiped it away impatiently.

"I still don't know if I'm ready to see him."

"You don't have to decide today," Brittany said. "You do have to decide if you want to go the rest of your life with this giant question mark in your chest."

That landed.
Hard.

Ava took a long, shaky breath.

"I hate when you're right," she muttered. Brittany smiled faintly. "It's a burden."

They sat in silence for a minute, the only sound the hum of the fridge and the faint TV noise from the living room.

"How long do you have left on your month?" Brittany asked quietly.

"Ten days," Ava said. Brittany nodded. "Do you want to use them here... or get your life back in Seattle?"

The word *back* made something flicker behind Ava's ribs.

Her bed.
Her plants.
Her tiny desk and the way the afternoon light hit it just right.

And, inevitably, the image of Cole in her kitchen, barefoot and laughing at her coffee machine.

"I think..." Ava started, then trailed off. Brittany waited.

"I think I need to go home," Ava said finally. "Not to him. Not yet. Just... to my own space. To see if I still want him when I'm not broken and hiding."

"That is an extremely emotionally mature answer," Brittany declared. "I am both proud and slightly offended."

Ava snorted weakly. "Why are you offended?"

"Because you're outgrowing your chaos era," Brittany said. "What am I supposed to do for entertainment?"

Ava rolled her eyes, but the smile lingered.

"What about Nick?" she asked. "He's still at my place."

"We'll kick him out," Brittany said breezily. "He can go home and annoy my mom instead."

"Does he know?" she asked softly. Brittany made a face. "Oh yeah. He called me immediately. Like, 'Uh, sis? Your boy showed up drunk at Ava's door, and I don't know what to do about it.'"

Ava's heart stuttered.

"He came to my apartment?"

"Yeah," Brittany said. "Nick said he looked like a kicked puppy. A big, sad, very polite puppy that insisted on leaving because he 'promised to give you space.'"

A sound escaped Ava that wasn't quite a sob and wasn't quite a laugh.

She covered her face with her hands.

"Of course he did."

"Look," Brittany said, gentling again. "No one is saying you owe him forgiveness. But I think you owe yourself the truth. And right now, the truth is sitting in Seattle in an apartment he rented big enough for both of you, thinking he lost you."

Ava's throat burned.

"Pros and cons?" she whispered.

"Hit me," Brittany said immediately, pulling a notebook toward them.

Ava stared at the blank page for a second. Then started.

"Pros of talking to him," she said quietly. "One: I get answers." Brittany wrote it down.

"Two: I stop filling in the blanks with the worst possible scenario."

"Three," Brittany added, "if he's as in love with you as I think, you get your guy back."

Ava glared at her.

"Fine, I'll put that in the 'potential pro, do not read out loud' category," Brittany muttered, scribbling.

"Cons," Ava said, voice softer. "One: he could say something that hurts more."

"Two: it might not fix anything," Brittany said.

"Three," Ava whispered, "if I'm wrong again, I don't know if I can come back from it."

Brittany stopped writing.

"You're not the only one in this relationship who gets to be brave," she said. "He's already moved his entire life. Maybe let him show up for this part, too."

Ava stared at the list.

Pros and cons, fear and hope, all jumbled together in messy handwriting.

She thought about the way his voice had sounded on the phone. The texts from the airport. The way he'd said *I'm not him.*

Her fingers curled around the edge of the table.

"Okay," she said finally. "I'll go home at the end of the week."

Britt's eyes brightened. "Okay."

"And..." Ava swallowed. "I'll text him. Not now. But... soon." Brittany nodded like a therapist who'd just gotten the answer she'd been patiently extracting for thirty minutes.

"Good," she said. "You don't have to set a date. You have to open a door."

Ava's stomach flipped.

Later that night, after Mrs. Mills had gone to bed and Zach was half-asleep on the couch with a game on, Ava sat alone in the guest room, her phone in hand.

The room was quiet.
Her heart was not.

She opened her message thread with Cole for the first time in weeks.

The last thing was his long, raw text from the airport.

She reread it.
Her eyes burned.

Her thumbs hovered over the keyboard. Dozens of drafts flashed through her head.

I'm sorry.
I miss you.
I'm not ready.
I don't know what I want.

She deleted all of them.
Started again.

Finally, she typed.

We should talk, my place. I'll let you know when.

She stared at the little block of text.

It wasn't forgiveness.
It wasn't a promise.
It was a possibility.

Her hands shook as she hit send.
The message left with a soft whoosh.

She exhaled like she'd been holding her breath for three weeks.

On the other side of the country, in a too-big apartment with half-unpacked boxes, Cole's phone buzzed on the counter.

He glanced over absently.
Then did a double-take.

The glass of water in his hand trembled just a little as he read the notification.

Ava Harper: We should talk, my place. I'll let you know when.

For a long moment, he didn't move.
Didn't breathe.

Then, slowly, like someone rewinding a heartbeat, his shoulders dropped.

Not over.
Not yet.

He didn't reply.
He wouldn't push.

He just set the phone down carefully, like it was something fragile, and leaned both hands on the counter.

"Okay," he whispered to the empty room.

"Whenever you're ready."

CHAPTER THIRTY

Ava was halfway through folding the last of her laundry, clean, New York-washed clothes ready to be packed for her flight home, when her phone buzzed with an unknown number.

She almost ignored it.

Unknown numbers meant telemarketers. Or HR. Or her doctor, reminding her she was overdue for a checkup, she had zero emotional bandwidth to deal with.

But something prickled the back of her neck.

She picked it up.

"Hello?"

A sharp inhale came through the line.

Then—

"Is this Ava? Ava Harper?"

Ava froze.

She knew that voice. Soft southern, slightly dramatic, with a "I get what I want, and I talk fast doing it" cadence.

"...Emery," Ava said flatly.

On the other side of the line came a choked sound of relief. "Oh, thank God—okay, hi, sorry uh, I know this is weird, I know I'm the absolute last person you want calling, but—"

Ava sat on the edge of the bed.
She didn't say anything.

Emery steamrolled right over the silence.

"Look—I'm just gonna say this before you hang up on me because honestly? You should. You absolutely should. But I'm begging, no, literally begging, give me like sixty seconds before you block my entire bloodline."

Ava blinked slowly.

"...okay."

"Okay? Right. So, I messed up." Emery took a breath so big that Ava could hear her lungs expand. "No, scratch that, I catastrophically, systemically, epically messed up. Like if there were awards for emotional sabotage, I would win in all categories."

Ava raised an eyebrow.
Emery kept going.

"I knew you were at the door. I knew. And I, God, I hate myself for this. I wanted to scare you off. Because I thought he was leaving for you. And I thought, if I just delayed you, if I just... threw a wrench in the moment, he might reconsider."

Her voice cracked. "And it was selfish. And ugly. And absolutely none of your fault."

Ava still said nothing.
Emery rushed on, frantic and unraveling.

"And before you say it—I know. I know it wasn't my place. I know he's not my kid or my emotional support pet or whatever weird codependent nonsense I've been pulling since we were kids, but he's my brother. And I thought if he left, I'd lose him. Which is stupid, because he already left. He grew up. He moved on. And I just—didn't."

Her breath hitched. Ava stared at the laundry pile, calm as a lake.

Meanwhile, Emery sounded like she was pacing barefoot across hot coals.

"He hasn't talked to me, Ava. Not one text. Not even a passive-aggressive meme. Do you understand? My brother once texted me a full paragraph about a lizard in our backyard, but now? Nothing."

Ava had to bite her lip to keep from smiling. Emery barreled forward, unaware.

"He moved without telling me the day or the time. Brittany told me I deserved a timeout like a toddler. Do you know how humiliating that is? I'm thirty-six!"

Ava's heart squeezed, but she stayed silent.

"So," Emery continued, desperation rising, "I started digging and asking. And bothering literally everyone he knows because I needed to fix this before he cuts me out of the family Christmas card. And that's when I found out—he's not talking to anyone. Because of what I did."

Ava exhaled slowly.
But she still didn't speak.

She Let her sweat.
Let her empty every frantic word.
Let her feel the consequences.

"I just, Ava—I am so goddamn sorry," Emery said finally, voice trembling. "I didn't think. I didn't consider your feelings. Or his. I didn't consider anything except my own fear. And I know you have no reason to trust me. I know you probably think our whole family is toxic. I know you think I'm some jealous ex or whatever—"

"Emery."

Dead stop.
Ava's voice was quiet.

Calm.
Measured.

"You're his sister. I know."

A tiny squeak came through the receiver. "B-Brittany told you?"

"No," Ava said. "Brittany showed me your Instagram."

A strangled groan. "Oh God. Did she show you the braces? Or the leather bracelet era? Please tell me she skipped the leather bracelet era—"

"She did not skip it."

Emery made a noise like she wanted to fling herself into the sun.

Ava waited.

Emery sucked in a breath. "So, you know I wasn't... you know. With him. Like that."

"Yes."

"So, you know he wasn't cheating on you."

"...yes."

"So, you know I'm just an emotionally stunted disaster who projected all her abandonment issues onto a surprise visit?"

Ava's lips twitched. "Yes."

Another pause.

"Wait." Emery's voice sharpened. "If you *know* all that, then why are you still hiding on the opposite side of the country?"

Ava smiled faintly.

"I'm not hiding."

"Could've fooled me!" Emery snapped—then immediately backpedaled. "Sorry, sorry, that was rude—I'm not supposed to be rude, I'm supposed to be groveling—"

"Emery?"

"Yes?"

"I already texted him."

Silence.
Then—

"You what?"

Ava almost laughed.

"I texted him."

"What did you say? Did you apologize? Did you yell at him? Did you tell him you're coming back? Did you—"

"It was short," Ava said.

We should talk at my place. I'll let you know when.

The gasp that came through the phone was violent.

"Oh my God, Ava—that's basically a proposal."

"It is not."

"It is," Emery insisted. "In my family, 'we should talk' is one step above 'should I bring a casserole to meet your parents?'"

Ava rolled her eyes.

"Emery," she said softly, "I'm not done with him."

The other end of the line went quiet.

Then: "...good."

Ava's throat tightened.

"He hurt me," she whispered.

"And you scared the shit out of him," Emery replied. "Seems even to me."

Ava snorted before she could stop herself.

Emery softened.

"For what it's worth... he loves you. He loves you like an absolute idiot. The kind of idiot who carried your favorite coffee mug across three states and ate bran flakes for dinner because he couldn't make himself grocery shop without you."

Ava stared down at her hands.
Yeah. She'd figured as much.

"Thank you for calling," she said finally.

"Thank you for listening," Emery replied. "And Ava?"

"Yeah?"

"Please don't break his heart again. He's awful at pretending he's fine."

Ava let out a shaky breath.

"Yeah," she whispered. "So am I."

They ended the call.

Ava sat still for a long moment, phone warm against her palm, the soft hum of Brittany's mom's house grounding her.

She wasn't fixed.
She wasn't whole.

But she was ready.
Three more days.

Then Seattle.
Then her apartment.
Then the door she'd opened with a message.

Whatever happened next, she wouldn't run from it.

CHAPTER THIRTY-ONE

Ava had never packed so slowly in her life.

Her suitcase lay open on Brittany's old bedroom floor, already half full. She sat cross-legged beside it, rolling a T-shirt and then unrolling it again like that would somehow delay the inevitable.

Three weeks ago, she'd arrived at this house in pieces.

Now she was… still cracked, still careful, but at least held together with something sturdier than panic.

Her phone buzzed on the bed beside her.

Brittany: u almost ready? Mom is threatening to pack for u, and u know what that means.

Ava shuddered.

Last time Mrs. Mills had "helped" pack, Ava had arrived back at college with three pairs of pajama pants and exactly one actual shirt.

Ava: On it. Tell her I like my dignity.

A second later, a shout floated down the hallway.

Mrs. Mills shouted down the hall, "Your dignity is overrated. Socks are not."

Ava cracked a smile despite the knot in her stomach.

She tucked the last sweater into her suitcase, zipped it closed, and sat back on her heels.

Okay.
She was really doing this.

Going back.
Going home.

Back to Seattle.
Back to her studio.
Back to... him.

Her phone buzzed again.
This time it wasn't Brittany.

Flight Reminder: Departure three hours.

Her chest squeezed.

[Ava]: Right. No backing out now.

She stood, wiped sweaty palms on her leggings, and dragged her suitcase into the hallway.

Brittany leaned against the wall, arms crossed, watching her with eyes that were both soft and sharp.

"You look like you're going to your execution," she observed.

"Feels like it," Ava muttered.

Brittany straightened and took the suitcase handle from her. "You're going home. Not to a firing squad."

"Debatable."

Brittany bumped her shoulder. "You texted him. He knows you want to talk. That's huge."

Ava's stomach flipped at the memory.

We should talk. My place. I'll let you know when.

Her thumb had hovered over send for so long she thought her phone might time her out of courage altogether.

But she'd done it.
Tiny miracle.

Now she had to follow through.

"I still don't know what I'm going to say," she admitted quietly.

"Good," Brittany said.

Ava blinked. "How is that good?"

"Because if you scripted the whole thing," Brittany said, "you'd sound like a robot, and he'd think you were breaking up with him again."

Ava grimaced. "...fair."

"Just tell the truth," Brittany said. "Even the messy parts. Especially the messy parts. He can handle it."

"I'm not worried about him handling it," Ava said. "I'm worried about me handling it."

Brittany's expression softened.

"You already did the hard part, you know," she said. "You stayed. You felt everything. You didn't shut down and run from yourself."

Ava let that sink in.
Stayed.

She hadn't thought of it like that before.

"I'm still going to throw up," she informed the room.

"That's valid," Mrs. Mills said, appearing from the kitchen with a travel mug and a Ziploc full of snacks. "Here. For the plane."

Ava took the bag.

Inside: granola bars, crackers, and the fancy gummy bears Mrs. Mills hid from Brittany.

Her throat tightened.

"Thank you," she said, and meant more than just for the snacks.

Mrs. Mills reached up to cup her cheek.

"You call if you need anything," she said. "Middle of the night, middle of the day, middle of an existential crisis, I'm here."

Ava's eyes burned.
She nodded.

Zach's voice floated in from the front door. "If we don't leave now, you're going to meet your gate from the outside of the plane."

"Coming," Ava called.

Brittany wrapped her in a hug so tight it squeezed air out of her.

"Don't chicken out," she murmured into Ava's hair.

"I won't," Ava whispered back.

"Promise?"

"Promise."

Brittany leaned back, searching her face like she could see each thought scrolling through.

Then she smiled. "Okay. Let's go give Delta more of our money."

The airport felt different this time.

Less like an emergency exit, more like a fork in the road, she was choosing instead of being shoved down.

She and Zach walked her to the security line. Brittany had insisted on coming too, of course, standing on the "no ticket" side of the rope and glaring at the TSA agent as if they might personally hurt her best friend.

"Text when you get to the gate," Zach said. "And when you land. And when you get home. And after you eat something that isn't airport food."

"That's excessive," Ava said.

"That's love," Brittany corrected.

Ava rolled her eyes and hugged them both again, one at a time.

"Tell your mom thank you," she said.

"You brought half her Tupperware back," Brittany said. "She's already forgiven you for everything."

Ava laughed, then had to step forward as the line moved.

Brittany walked along the rope beside her until the metal detector got in the way.

"Hey," Brittany called, cupping her hands around her mouth. "Harper!"

Ava turned, backpack slung over one shoulder.

"You've got this," Brittany said, loud enough for the whole line to hear. "And if he doesn't grovel appropriately, I *will* fly out there and supervise."

Ava's face burned. People in line glanced between them with faint amusement.

"Thank you for that," she muttered once she'd shuffled a few feet farther.

"You're welcome!" Brittany chirped, absolutely unbothered.

Ava waved one last time and stepped through security. No alarms, no pat-down, just the usual indignity of removing her shoes in public.

At the gate, she found an empty seat near the window and sank down.

Her phone buzzed almost immediately.

Brittany: Already proud of you. Also, I'm stalking ur flight on the app.

Ava smiled.
She opened another thread.

Cole.

Her last message sat there like a quiet heartbeat.

We should talk at my place. I'll let you know when.

He hadn't replied.
She'd told him not to.

Still, some petty part of her had hoped for an "okay" or a thumbs-up or an emoji or anything that said *I'm still here*.

She traced the edge of her phone with her thumb.

In a few hours, they'd be in the same city again.

Same time zone.
Same sky.

The gate agent announced pre-boarding.

Ava closed her eyes for a moment and took a slow, deliberate breath.

[Ava]: You're not flying back to breakup. You're flying back to find out if this can be put back together.

The distinction mattered.

She stood when her group was called, shuffled down the jet bridge with everyone else, and found her seat by the window.

Her brain replayed flashes of another flight, her to New York, crying into airplane air and refusing to look at her phone.

This time, she stared straight ahead, planted her feet, and held onto herself instead of the armrest.

Baby steps.
Still progress.

Clouds rolled beneath the plane like mountains of cotton.

Ava leaned her forehead against the window and let the white blur steady her.

She didn't open her laptop.
She didn't answer the growing pile of pings.

She spent the first hour of the flight doing nothing but breathing and imagining both possible futures.

Future A: She talked to Cole, it went horribly, and they awkwardly coexisted in the same city as coworkers who once almost had something real.

Future B: She talked to Cole, it didn't fix everything instantly, but it opened a door they could walk through together.

Future A made her stomach twist.
Future B made her chest ache.

The flight attendant appeared at her elbow with a plastic cup of ginger ale.

"On the house," she said with a little conspiratorial smile. "You look like you're thinking too hard."

Ava huffed out a breath. "That obvious?"

"Only to professionals," the woman said, tapping her name badge. "We see everything."

Ava accepted the drink.

Ginger ale used to be her heartbreak beverage of choice. Breakups, bad days, stomach-clenching anxiety, it all tasted like artificial ginger and airline ice cubes.

She took a sip.
It still tasted like nerves.
But less like freefall.

More like standing on a cliff and choosing whether to jump.

Seattle greeted her with gray skies and a wind that cut straight through her jacket.

The familiarity of it hit her harder than she expected.

The same dingy carpet in the terminal. The same too-bright advertisement for coffee she'd never actually tried, the same cluster of people waiting by the arrivals sign.

She scanned the crowd out of reflex.

For a split second, she imagined Cole there, hands shoved in pockets, shoulders tense, trying to look casual and failing spectacularly.

He wasn't.
Of course, he wasn't.

She hadn't told him when she was landing. She wasn't ready for another airport scene.

Her phone buzzed as she stepped out past baggage claim.

Nick: I'm by the rideshare pickup. Silver Subaru, I made a sign, but Zach said it was too much, so I left it at home.

Ava smiled despite herself.
A minute later, she spotted the car.

Nick leaned across the passenger seat and flung open the door.

"Get in, loser," he said. "We're going through emotional healing."

"That's not how the quote goes," she said, climbing in.

"Close enough."

He pulled away from the curb with far too much enthusiasm for someone who'd admitted last week that he still sometimes missed turns in his own neighborhood.

They drove in silence for a few minutes, the city sliding back into view.

Familiar streets. Familiar skyline.
Her chest squeezed.

"So," Nick said eventually, drumming his fingers on the steering wheel. "How's New York?"

"Cold," she said. "Loud. Full of Mills women trying to feed me my feelings."

Nick snorted. "Sounds right."

He glanced over at her.

"You look better," he said. "Less like you're about to detach your soul and move to the woods."

"That's a specific image."

"Britt sent pictures," he said. "The ones of you before waffles? Terrifying."

Ava made a face.

"She also told me about the text," Nick added, more cautiously. "To Cole."

A spark of embarrassment flickered in her chest.

"Of course she did," Ava muttered.

"Hey." Nick's voice gentled. "I think it's good."

Her fingers twisted in the strap of her bag. "I don't know if it's good yet."

"Yeah," he said. "But it's not nothing."

They fell quiet again as the car merged onto the freeway.

Rain hit the windshield in light, intermittent taps.

When they finally pulled up outside her building, Ava's heart lodged somewhere near her throat.

From the sidewalk, her studio looked the same.

Same narrow window.
Same little potted plant on the sill that Nick had apparently kept alive.

She swallowed.

"Place is all yours again," Nick said, cutting the engine. "I washed the sheets. Didn't touch your drawers. Only mildly judged your Tupperware situation."

Ava let out a shaky laugh.

"Thank you," she said. "For staying. For... being there that night."

Nick shrugged like it was nothing.

"Couldn't exactly let my sister's best friend emotionally implode alone," he said. "Plus, this place has better water pressure than my apartment."

She smiled. Her hand hovered on the door handle.

"You got this," Nick said quietly.

She nodded, throat tight.

"Text Brittany" he added. "She's pretending not to hover, but she's absolutely hovering."

"I will."

"And, uh..." He scratched the back of his neck. "When you do talk to him, tell him I said he owes me one for not punching him the night he showed up drunk here."

Ava blinked. "You were going to punch him?"

"Very gently," Nick said. "Emotionally."

She rolled her eyes.

"Bye, Nick."

"Bye, Ava."

She stepped out into the damp Seattle air and watched his car pull away.

Then she turned toward the building.

Every step up the stairwell felt like walking backward through time.

She reached her door.

Her fingers shook as she slid the key in the lock. The door opened with its familiar soft scrape.

She stepped inside.

Her tiny studio greeted her like a held breath finally released.

Same bed in the corner.
Same little table under the window.
Same too small kitchenette.

A faint hint of Nick's cologne lingered, mixed with her own detergent.

Ava dropped her bag just inside the door and stood there, taking it in.

This was where she'd sat on the floor and cried after Nathan, where she'd taken the job that brought her to Cole's team. Where she'd logged in, day after day, to see his face smiling at her through a webcam.

It had been a refuge.
Then a trap.
Now, it could be a starting point.

She walked to the window and pressed her fingers against the cold glass.

Seattle blurred beyond it, gray and familiar and hers.

Her phone felt heavy in her pocket.
She pulled it out.

No new messages from him.
Of course not.

She hadn't given him anything to respond to.
Her thumb hovered over their thread.

We should talk at my place. I'll let you know when. She could wait until tomorrow.

Until she unpacked.
Until she'd slept.

Until she'd had one night in her own bed without her heart trying to hammer out of her chest.

Or— Or she could take one small step.

Her fingers moved before she could talk herself out of it.

Ava: I'm back in Seattle.

She stared at the message for half a second.

Then hit send.

The whoosh felt louder in the quiet apartment than it had any right to.

Across town, in an apartment she hadn't seen yet, Cole's phone buzzed on a counter between two half-unpacked boxes.

He reached for it on instinct.
Saw her name.

And for the first time in weeks, let himself hope without immediately shutting it down.

Back in her studio, Ava set the phone on the little table and sank down onto the edge of her bed.

No reply came right away.
She didn't expect one.

She lay back, staring at the ceiling she'd memorized every crack of, and let the familiar creaks and hums of the building settle around her.

For better or worse, she was home.
Tomorrow, or the next day, they'd talk.
Tonight, she just had to do one thing.

Stay.

In her body.
In her city.

In the possibility that this didn't have to be the end.

Her eyes finally drifted closed.

Outside, the rain tapped gently against the window.

Seattle sighed.
And somewhere not far away, so did he.

CHAPTER THIRTY-TWO

Ava didn't sleep.
Not really.

She drifted in and out—light, restless half dreams where she kept imagining someone knocking on her door, or her phone vibrating with his name, or opening her eyes to find Cole sitting on the floor beside her bed waiting for her to wake up.

When the morning light finally pushed through her curtains, she felt wrung out and hollow, but steady.

Today was the day.

Not the conversation day, not yet, but the day she'd tell him *when*.

And maybe that was scarier.

She peeled herself out of bed, showered, pulled on soft leggings and a sweater, and made tea in her tiny kitchen. The familiarity of the routine helped a little.

Her studio looked different in the daylight. Smaller, somehow. Like the walls had crept closer in while she'd been gone.

Nick had left it tidy, but it was still her one-room box of a life, a life she had carved out alone. A life she'd been proud of, once.

Now it felt like a dorm room compared to the life she wanted. Compared to the life that was waiting across the city.

She sat at her small table, staring at her laptop, pretending she was capable of work. She answered two emails, stared at a spreadsheet she didn't process, and finally closed the lid.

Her mind was too loud.

[Ava]: What am I going to say? What if he says the wrong thing? What if I break again? What if I don't?

She exhaled shakily.
Her phone buzzed.

Brittany: Do not ghost him. Do not overthink. Drink water u dehydrated fern.

Ava smirked. Typical Brittany. Right on schedule.

Ava: Working on it kind of.

Brittany: Nick said u looked like a haunted raccoon at the airport. Rude but probably accurate.

Ava: I hate u.

Brittany: no u don't update me when u send the message not if don't u dare pull a vanishing act.

Ava locked her phone.

She wasn't going to vanish.
Not this time.

By late afternoon, her anxiety cleaning had reached a fever pitch.

She reorganized her utensils.
She wiped down her kitchenette.
She refolded the already-folded shirts in her dresser. She swept the floor even though it didn't need sweeping.

At 3:12 p.m., she caught herself alphabetizing her spice jars and groaned.

"Get a grip," she muttered.

She walked to the bed, sank down on it, and pulled her phone into her lap.

Cole's message thread was still open.
Her stomach did a slow, fluttering twist.
She reread her last message to him.

I'm back in Seattle.

He had seen it. She could tell by the subtle shift in the read receipt timing.

But he hadn't replied.

Good. She had told him not to jump in. She

had told him she'd be the one to say when.

This was on her.

And the longer she put it off, the worse her heartbeat felt in her throat.

She inhaled, slow and steady.

Then typed.

Ava: Tomorrow after work. Come over.

She stared at the message.
Two lines.

Simple.
Clear.
She hovered.

Inside her chest, fear and hope braided together so tightly she couldn't tell them apart.

"Send it," she whispered to herself.

She did.
The message flew off her screen.

Her pulse hammered.
Her phone stayed silent.

She set it face down before she could spiral.

Across the city, Cole sat on the floor of his half-unpacked apartment, surrounded by cardboard boxes and a takeout container he'd forgotten to finish.

He was scrolling aimlessly through Teams conversations, through stupid memes Zach had sent, through a recipe for baked chicken he wasn't going to make, just trying to keep his hands busy.

His phone buzzed.

He didn't look right away. He couldn't handle another spam email from some moving company or a reminder from a furniture delivery service.

Then he saw her name light up the screen. Everything inside him stopped.

Ava Harper: Tomorrow after work. Come over.

He exhaled so sharply he had to put a hand to his chest.

His heart was doing something wild, like it wanted to run, collapse, fly, and hide all at once.

He didn't reply.
He wouldn't reply.

She needed to lead this part.
But he closed his eyes and whispered.

"Okay. I'll be there."

CHAPTER THIRTY-THREE

The next day crawled by.

Ava tried working, emphasis on *tried*.

She logged into meetings, nodded at screens, typed things she immediately had to delete because they made no sense, and drank so much tea her stomach sloshed.

Every hour, she checked the wall clock over her tiny kitchenette. Every hour, the hands barely moved.

By 4:45 p.m., she was pacing her entire studio, six steps from the door to the window, turn, and six steps back.

Her phone was on the table.
Face up.

Mocking her with its silence.

5:02 p.m., a buzz.
Her breath caught—

No. Teams alert.

She turned it off. She didn't want to hear from anyone except one single person.

She brushed her hair twice.
Changed her shirt three times.

Rearranged the blanket on her bed four times.

Put on lip balm. Took it off. Put it on again.

5:28 p.m.

She checked her reflection in her microwave door because her studio didn't have a full-length mirror.

She looked pale.
Wide-eyed.

Like someone standing on the edge of something huge.

5:31 p.m..

A knock.
She froze.

Her lungs forgot their job. Her hands went cold. Her heartbeat crawled up into her throat.

The knock came again, gentler this time.

"Ava?" Cole's voice. Muffled. Careful. Terrified.

Her knees weakened.

[Ava]: Okay. I can do this.

She walked to the door, fingers trembling on the knob.

She opened it.
There he was.

Cole. Jeans and a gray sweatshirt. Clean-shaven except for that tiny shadow on his jaw. Hair a little messy, like he'd run his hands through it fifty times. Eyes soft and scared and so full of her she almost forgot how to stand.

"Hi," he said quietly.

Her grip tightened on the doorframe. "Hi."

They stared at each other for a long, suspended heartbeat. Then she stepped aside.

"Come in."

He did.
Slowly.

Like he didn't want to overwhelm the space.

Like he didn't want to overwhelm *her*.

He glanced around her studio—a small table, bed, kitchenette, single window, and swallowed.

"You've been here a long time," he murmured, quietly reverent.

"Yeah," she said.

He nodded, then stood there, unsure of what to do with his hands, his body, and his breath.

Ava gestured toward the small table by the window. "Sit?"

He sat. She sat across from him.

It felt like miles between them, even though the table was barely two feet wide.

For a moment, neither spoke.
Then Ava inhaled and began.

"I need to start with something honest," she said. "And it's... embarrassing."

Cole straightened, eyes locked on hers.

"Anything," he said. "I'm right here."

She swallowed.

"When I saw her—when I saw Emery—I didn't see your sister. I saw... something else. Something from before you. Someone who hurt me." Her throat tightened. "I didn't choose to have that reaction. It just happened. It was like my brain short-circuited."

Cole's expression softened—painful, tender, apologetic all at once.

"Ava..."

"No," she said gently, lifting a hand. "Let me get through this part."

He nodded.
She continued.

"I panicked. And when I panic, I run. That's

my flaw. It's the worst one. And I know it hurt you. I know disappearing wasn't fair. I know it made you think I didn't trust you." Her voice thinned. "And I'm sorry. Truly."

His eyes glistened.
He didn't speak yet.

She kept going.

"I needed time to get out of my own head. And I'm not proud of how much time I took. But I'm here now. And I'm not running anymore."

She finally looked at him.
Really looked.

His jaw was tight.
His eyes were wet.
His shoulders held weeks of tension.

Then he exhaled, shaky.

"My turn?" he asked.

She nodded.

Cole leaned forward, elbows on his knees, palms pressed together like he was holding something fragile between them.

"I should've told you Emery was there," he said softly. "I should've warned you, even if she was just staying the night. Even if I didn't think it would cause issues. I should've said something."

Ava blinked. Opening her mouth to say something. He continued before she could speak.

"I was scared," he said, voice thinning. "But hiding things doesn't protect anyone. It just leaves gaps where fear grows."

Her chest ached.
Cole swallowed hard.

"And then when I realized why you were upset—why you left—God, Ava, I felt sick." His voice cracked. "Because I didn't protect you from the thing that scared you most. I didn't protect what we were building."

She pressed her hand to her chest.

"Cole..."

He looked up at her, eyes raw.

"I'm not mad at you for panicking," he whispered. "I'm mad at myself for letting you think, even for a second, that you were unloved or unwanted or replaceable."

Her eyes stung.

"I didn't think I was replaceable," she whispered. "I thought I was stupid."

"You weren't," he said. "You aren't. You saw something your brain recognized as danger, and you reacted like anyone who's been hurt before." He ran a shaky hand through his hair. "If anything, I should've run after you sooner."

"You did," she said, voice trembling. "You did run after me."

He laughed, breathless. "Not fast enough."

"Cole—"

"Ava," he said, voice breaking open. "I thought I lost you. I thought you were gone for good. And it was the worst, I mean the *worst*—feeling I've ever had."

A tear slipped down her cheek.

She reached across the table and touched his fingers.

He froze.

Then he turned his hand over and held hers.

Not tightly.
Not desperately.
Just… held.

"I'm here," she said softly.

He inhaled sharply. Then his thumb brushed the back of her hand, slow and reverent.

"Do you still want this?" he whispered.

Everything in her stilled.

"Yes," she said. No hesitation. No fear. Just truth. "I want you."

He closed his eyes like he'd been underwater for weeks and finally surfaced.

When he opened them again, the whole world was in them.

"Come here," he murmured.

She stood.
He stood.

They met halfway around the table, bodies close but not yet touching.

Ava lifted a hand to his jaw, feeling the faint stubble beneath her fingers.

Cole's breath caught.

"Ava..." he whispered.

And she kissed him.

Slow.
Deep.
Careful.

Hungry but careful.

Like rediscovering something she'd almost talked herself out of believing was real.

He kissed her back with so much relief she felt it in her whole body.

His hands slid to her waist, not pulling her in, just holding her like she was something sacred.

She pressed closer.
He exhaled against her lips.

The kiss deepened.
Soft turned to warm.
Warm turned to need.

He pulled back just enough to search her face, breath uneven, eyes dark with a question he didn't have to voice.

She answered by cupping his face between both hands, steady and certain, drawing him back to her.

His forehead dropped to hers, a quiet pause heavy with intention.

Then he walked her backward, slowly, gently until the backs of her legs met the edge of the bed.

They undressed each other like a conversation. Hesitant touches, shared breaths, soft laughter when her sweater got caught on her elbow, whispered apologies when his fingers trembled.

There was nothing frantic.
Nothing rushed.

Just two people who had spent years wanting this moment and were finally allowing themselves to touch each other without fear.

When they finally came together, Ava felt something inside her settle.

Not excitement.
Not adrenaline.
Not panic.

Something steadier.

Peace.
Belonging.
Home.

His mouth on her shoulder.
Her hands in his hair.

The soft sound he made when she pulled him closer. The way he murmured her name like a prayer.

Afterward, they lay tangled beneath her thin apartment blankets, his chest rising and falling beneath her cheek.

He kissed the top of her head.

"Aves?" he whispered.

"Hm?"

"I'm not going anywhere."

She closed her eyes.

"Good," she said softly. "Because neither am I."

They fell asleep like that—skin to skin, breaths syncing, the storm finally quiet.

Tomorrow, they would talk about the future.

They would start building something real. But right now?

Right now, they were enough. They were home.

CHAPTER THIRTY-FOUR

Ava woke slowly.

Warm.
Weighted.
Safe.

There was a solid arm around her waist, a quiet breath against the back of her neck, and the steady rise and fall of a body that was unmistakably Cole.

For a moment, she didn't move—just listened.

To him.
To the rain outside.
To the soft hum of her building.

To the quiet part of herself that finally, finally wasn't afraid.

When she shifted slightly, his arm tightened instinctively.

"Aves," he murmured, voice gravelly and sleep-drenched.

Her pulse fluttered.

"Morning," she whispered.

He pressed his face into her shoulder with a soft groan. "Should be illegal to wake up this good."

She smiled into her pillow.

They stayed like that for a while. Warm skin, soft breaths, no noise except the rhythm of being in the same bed for the first time after so many almosts.

Eventually, she rolled over.

Cole's eyes were half-open, messy hair falling over his forehead, expression soft in a way she'd never seen outside a webcam glitch.

He lifted a hand and brushed a thumb across her cheek.

"You okay?" he asked, quiet and sincere. "Really okay?"

Ava nodded, then took his hand and pressed it to her lips.

"I'm good," she said. "Better than good."

Relief washed over his face.

"Me too," he whispered.

He leaned in and kissed her—gentle, morning-warm, grounding. She curled her arm around him, pulling him a little closer.

When they finally separated, he glanced around her tiny studio.

There wasn't much to look at.

She followed his gaze—the bed pressed into one corner, the kitchenette squeezed into the other, the table beneath the window that held exactly two chairs and exactly zero elbow room.

His eyes softened.

"You've made it homey," he said carefully. "But... it's small."

"Very small," she agreed.

He swallowed, clearly choosing every word with care. "You know I'm not saying that as a critique. I just—"

"I know," she said. "It served a purpose. But I think I outgrew it without noticing."

Cole looked at her for a long moment. Then, with the gentlest tone she'd ever heard from him, he said.

"You don't have to stay here anymore."

Her breath caught.
He continued quietly and steadily.

"I have an apartment with space. With actual counters and full-sized furniture and a real bed frame and a second bedroom I absolutely didn't need but got anyway." His voice softened. "I thought... maybe one day... if things ever worked out, I wanted you to have the option."

Ava blinked.

"You chose your apartment because of me?"

He flushed. "Not... officially. But yeah."

Her lips parted.
He rushed to fill the silence.

"But there's no pressure. I'm not asking you to decide today, tomorrow, or even this month. I want you to know the door is open. Literally and—" He exhaled. "Figuratively."

Ava reached out and traced the line of his jaw.

"I want to move in."

His breath stuttered.

"Ava—"

"I don't want to wait a month," she said. "Or six. Or a year. I want to move into your apartment. With you."

A moment of stunned stillness.
Then—

His face broke open with something indescribably soft.

"Are you sure?"

She nodded. "Yes."

He cupped her face with both hands and kissed her like he couldn't help it. When he pulled back, his forehead rested against hers.

"Okay," he whispered. "Okay."

Ava felt a smile stretch across her face.

"Now?" she teased.

Cole choked out a laugh. "Right now?"

She shrugged. "Why not? I don't own much."

"You own exactly two pots, three plates, and a bed that squeaks every time you breathe."

"It is a terrible bed," she admitted.

"I'm never letting you sleep on it again," he declared, scandalized. "You deserve orthopedic support."

She giggled.
He kissed her again.

Slow.
Sweet.
Certain.

They spent the late morning gathering her things—clothes, blankets, the two pots, the three plates, the handful of books she loved too much to part with, and the tiny plant Nick had kept alive.

It all fit into exactly four boxes. Cole carried them easily, making two trips to his car.

Before they left, Ava stood in the middle of her studio one last time.

The room felt different now.

Smaller.
Quieter.

Empty in a way that didn't hurt.

She touched the edge of her little table, the one she'd worked at for years.

"You were good to me," she whispered to the room. "But I'm ready for better."

Cole appeared in the doorway, holding her keys.

"You ready?" he asked.

She turned toward him.

The man she loved stood there, hopeful, soft-eyed, steady, and she felt her chest warm.

"Yeah," she said. "I'm ready."

His apartment was bigger, brighter, and cleaner.

Boxes were still half-unpacked, furniture still finding its place. It looked like a life in progress.

A life with room for someone else.

She stepped inside, inhaling the faint scent of laundry detergent and new carpet.

Cole set the last box down by the kitchen island.

Ava walked farther in.

Her fingers brushed the back of his living room chair.

The kitchen was much larger than the tiny one in her studio where they'd spent a week brushing past each other in the sweetest kind of chaos.

The big window overlooking the courtyard made the space feel open and unexpectedly calm.

"This is really nice," she murmured.

He stepped beside her.

"It was missing something," he said.

[Cole]: You.

He didn't say it out loud, but she felt it in every quiet inch of the room.

He reached for her hand.

"You're home now," he said softly.

She turned to him.

"Yeah," she whispered, leaning into his chest as his arms wrapped around her.

"I am."

They spent the afternoon unpacking her small collection of belongings into their space.

Her mugs next to his.
Her notebook on his desk.
Her toothbrush beside his in the bathroom.

Her clothes hanging in the closet, he'd intentionally left half-empty, just in case this day ever came.

Every placement felt like a soft promise.

A gentle beginning. A weaving of two lives instead of two threads running parallel.

At sunset, they collapsed onto his couch.
A real couch.

A comfortable, grown-up couch. A couch where two people could sit without knocking elbows.

Ava curled into his side.
Cole kissed her hair.

"Want takeout?" he asked.

"Starving," she said.

He grabbed his phone but paused, looking down at her, thumb tracing circles on her shoulder.

"Ava?"

"Yeah?"

"I'm really glad you came back."

She lifted her head and kissed him, slow and sure.

"So am I," she murmured against his lips.

She settled back against him, closing her eyes.

The city hummed outside. The apartment breathed around them. And for the first time in a long time—

Everything fit, felt right, and felt like home.

EPILOGUE

Six Months Later

The knock on the door came three seconds after Ava heard Brittany's squeal in the hallway.

"Ava! Open this door before I pee myself!"

Ava laughed and swung it open just in time for Brittany to waddle inside, one hand on her lower back, the other clutching a travel tote the size of a small country.

"You weren't kidding," Ava said, stepping back so Zach could drag in two suitcases behind his very pregnant wife.

"I have a tiny human karate kicking my bladder," Brittany announced. "Everything is urgent now."

Ava hugged her as gently as she could around the baby bump.

"You look amazing."

"I look like a beanbag," Brittany corrected. "A very emotional beanbag."

Zach slid an arm around her shoulders. "You look beautiful."

Brittany sniffed. "Shut up, I love you."

Ava smiled, watching them. Six months ago, she couldn't have imagined being here—comfortable, steady, living with Cole in an apartment that finally felt lived in.

Now she couldn't imagine anything else.

"Where's Cole?" Zach asked, setting the last suitcase down.

"Kitchen," Ava said. "He's trying to impress you with homemade breakfast tacos."

Zach grinned. "Finally. Someone else for me to judge."

They walked into the kitchen to find Cole standing over the stove, flipping tortillas like his life depended on it.

When he saw them, his whole face lit up. His amazing smile is shining.

"Hey!" he said, wiping his hands on a towel and going straight to Brittany for a gentle hug. "Look at you."

"If one more person tells me I'm glowing," she warned, "I'm biting them."

Cole raised both hands in surrender. "You're terrifying."

Zach clapped Cole on the back. "Good to see you, man."

"You too," Cole said, pulling him into a quick one-armed hug. "Welcome home."

Ava paused in the doorway, letting the moment wash over her.

Friends.
Family.
Warmth.

A home filled with people she loved.

This... was the life she'd been afraid to want.

She wandered into the kitchen, brushing past Cole to grab glasses from the cabinet. His hand slid to her waist instinctively, his thumb sweeping her hip in a familiar, quiet hello.

Six months of living together, and that tiny touch still melted her.

"Need help?" he murmured.

"No," she said. "Keep cooking. They're starving."

Brittany made a wounded noise as she walked back into the kitchen. "Rude but true."

Later, while Zach and Cole debated the structural integrity of breakfast tacos, and Brittany lay on the couch, insisting she wasn't napping (she was very much napping). Ava stepped onto the balcony with a fresh cup of tea.

Seattle stretched out below, gray clouds wrapped around the skyline, the faint smell of rain drifting past. Her city. Their home.

She wrapped both hands around the mug and breathed in.

A soft sliding sound came from behind her. The balcony door.

Cole stepped out, hands in his pockets, expression soft.

"You okay?" he asked.

"Yeah," she said. "Just... taking it in."

He leaned against the railing beside her, close enough that their arms brushed.

"You've been extra quiet today," he said gently.

"Good quiet," she promised.

He nodded.

For a moment, they just watched the slow drift of clouds. Comfortable. Steady. Full.

Then Cole cleared his throat.
Her stomach flipped.

He turned slightly, pocketing one hand but keeping the other free, thumb rubbing against his palm like he was bracing himself.

"I, uh..." He exhaled. "This isn't the smooth speech I practiced in my head."

Ava blinked.
His eyes found hers.
And everything in his face softened.

"Ava Harper," he said quietly, "I am stupidly, ridiculously, and hopelessly in love with you."

Her breath stilled.
He continued, voice rough around the edges.

"You're the best thing that's ever walked into my life. Even when you ran away," he added with a faint smile, "you still found your way back. And I—"

He swallowed. "I don't want there to be a version of my life that doesn't have you in it."

Ava's heartbeat stumbled.

Cole shifted, pulling something from his sweatshirt pocket.

Not a box.
No velvet.

Just a simple silver ring in his palm—sleek, minimal, elegant.

Exactly her.

"I didn't want to wait for a fancy restaurant or a coordinated surprise or anything that wasn't us," he said. "I wanted to do it here. At home. With you."

Her eyes blurred.

He held out the ring, hand shaking just slightly.

"Ava Grace Harper, will you marry me?"

Ava stared at him—this man who'd chased her, held her, forgiven her, chosen her, and felt something deep inside settle like a final puzzle piece clicking into place.

"Yes," she whispered.

Then louder, with a laugh that broke on a sob, "Yes."

Relief crashed over his face.

He slid the ring onto her finger with hands that trembled most endearingly.

The metal settled warm against her skin. A perfect fit.

Cole cupped her face and kissed her—slow, full, grateful, and she kissed him back with every piece of the life they'd built.

Behind them, from the living room, Brittany yelled. "Did you just get engaged without me?"

Ava laughed into Cole's chest.
He groaned.

Zach shouted, "I told you to wait until dinner!"

Brittany's footsteps thundered toward the balcony.

Ava smiled up at Cole, heart full.

"Ready?" she whispered.

"God, no," he said. "But I wouldn't choose anyone else to survive this with."

The door burst open.

Ava held out her hand, ring glinting in the gray Seattle light.

Brittany screamed.
Zach fist pumped.

Cole wrapped an arm around her waist like he couldn't believe she was real.

Ava looked at him, soft and certain.

No longer questioning.
No longer worried.

This time, she was home.

A NOTE FROM THE AUTHOR

Thank you for being here — truly.

This is my first novel, and the fact that you chose to spend your time with these pages, with Ava and Cole, with the little world I built one sentence at a time... it means more to me than you could ever know.

If this story made you smile, laugh, breathe easier, or feel a little less alone... then it did exactly what I hoped it would.

And if you, too, carry a story inside you — a half-formed idea, a whisper of a scene, a character who won't leave you alone — I hope you let this be your sign:

Your words matter.
Your voice matters.
Your story deserves a place in the world.

If I can finish a book, so can you. Keep going. Someone out there needs the story only you can tell.

From the bottom of my heart:
Thank you for reading.

— Elaine Lawrence